Rolling Thunder

The town, once a thriving and growing community, was now rotten and Tyler Holt the one man who could not be browbeaten lay dead, lynched by a mob. It was all down to Tom Quinn, the man who had led in the first settlers, to burn out the cancerous sore that Stratton had become. Worse still the surrounding land of Stratton Valley with its lush grass rightfully belonged to him.

But what could Tom do, facing as he did, the might of Peebles and his cohorts who controlled Stratton? Only his courage and gun skills could save the day.

Rolling Thunder

Owen G. Irons

A Black Horse Western

ROBERT HALE · LONDON

© Owen G. Irons 2007
First published in Great Britain 2007

ISBN 978-0-7090-8382-5

Robert Hale Limited
Clerkenwell House
Clerkenwell Green
London EC1R 0HT

Typeset by
Derek Doyle & Associates, Shaw Heath
Printed and bound in Great Britain by
Antony Rowe Limited, Wiltshire

ONE

It was a sad and miserable day made more miserable by the steady fall of the cold rain across the graveyard. The aspen trees clustering near to the plot trembled in the gusting wind. Tyler Holt, buried six feet deep in the ground, felt none of it, saw none of it.

Someone had burned his name into a flat piece of wood, using a poker iron or some such instrument, and tacked it to an upright pole at the head of the grave. The marker wouldn't last long, nor would memory of Tyler. But I stood there now, remembering him, as the heavy drops of rain fell, slapping at the black slicker I wore.

I heard the press of approaching footsteps against the debris of the untended graveyard and my hand dropped automatically to the walnut grips of my holstered Colt revolver. I did not draw in that split second as had once been my reflexive habit, and was relieved that I had not when I saw the person who was approaching, her face half-hidden under a dark-red hood, her mouth grim, her blue eyes unhappy and angry at once. I lowered my hand and waited for Mary Ford to approach me through the strengthening rain, her small boots tentative over the rough ground, her fists clenched.

'Don't do it, Tom,' she said, halting a yard from me, the rain screening her young face. 'Don't kill my brothers. It wasn't their doing despite what you may have heard.'

'I haven't heard anything except that Tyler was shot down by a mob,' I said. The gusting wind was rattling the branches of the forlorn trees now, and rivulets of cold water snaked down the slope of the tiny graveyard. Distantly, thunder boomed above the Rocky Mountain peaks, their heads hidden in the massed clouds.

'My brothers weren't there,' Mary said urgently. Her arms lifted slightly and for a moment her fingers stretched out as if she would take my sleeve. Her eyes searched mine, looking for belief. 'It was the whole town . . . that mob that went to Tyler's ranch and killed him.' She waited for my response. Lightning crackled behind her, illuminating her starkly, briefly, and then a second heavy peal of thunder rolled across the dark land.

'Please, Tom, don't kill Ben and William.'

'I didn't come back to kill your brothers, Mary,' I said, finding my throat tight as I looked into the eyes of the girl I had once loved and then lost. 'I've come to kill a town.'

The desk clerk at the Stratton Hotel looked like he was afraid to give me a room key, more afraid not to, when I entered the building, scarring the oak floor a little with my spurs in passing. I was dripping rainwater; the sky outside was dark, the lobby smelled of stale cigar smoke and vaguely of women's powder. I hardly paid any attention to the fat man behind the desk as he asked me to sign the hotel register. I was still thinking about the look in Mary's eyes as I walked past her, leaving her standing in the iron gray of the rain-swept day. It was horror I saw in them, it seemed. But a woman's eyes never express only a single emotion, and I thought for a moment I had seen a hint of her former caring. But it's not hard for a man to delude himself if he lets himself get caught up in blue eyes. I had walked away from her; it was for the best. You can't go back, a wise man had once told me.

But here I was – back in Stratton, Colorado

after a miserable week on the trail. I was back and by now all the town knew that Tom Quinn had returned and that he was still carrying his guns.

Something had gone wrong in this town. It had started out healthy and clean, breathing new life where there had been no civilization before. Now it seemed that a cancer had grown within it, dark and virulent. A group of dark riders had managed to threaten, bully and, almost with impunity, kill those who opposed them.

I knew this because I had guided the first settlers into the region, hemmed with tall stands of pine trees standing sentinel beside long, grassy valleys with sweet water running off the Pocono watercourse from the flanks of the Rocky Mountains, dividing into a dozen nourishing silver rills. I was proud to have brought families and hard-working young ranchers onto the hidden plateau that not many men had seen before. The land was plentiful and rich and the enterprising few I had led here had begun to build with youthful energy – a church, a school, stores and truck farms; a few cattle had been driven into the high valleys, enough to provide Stratton with all the beef it needed.

Then, from what I had heard, a man named Shelley Peebles had arrived. Looking out across the lush valleys, he realized he was looking at much more than a settlement, he was seeing land that could support thousands of head of steers with the deep grass and plentiful water. He began driving cattle up from Texas before he had purchased so much as an acre of land. With him he brought a dozen gunhands willing to ply their trade.

The settlers in the valley were forced to sell their small landholdings bit by bit. Those who refused to give up their hope for a new life in the West were harassed, burned out and sometimes shot out of hand on the feeblest of excuses.

Peebles had also brought along his own group of professional men – an attorney, a judge and a marshal who took office without opposition because there was no one among the young families willing or able to stand up and oppose him. Not with so many armed men willing to do Peebles's bidding for a few tainted dollars.

Tyler Holt, rest his soul, was one man who could not be ridden over. A Civil War veteran with four years of fighting behind him, his entire life spent struggling against the harshness of nature and men's ways, he had brought his wife, Sadie, and their three children to Stratton at my insistence. He thought he had found paradise in those high valleys where the peaceful wind drifted through the cedars and pines. He had taken my hand and shaken it firmly, his thanks reflected in his eyes beyond any words he could have spoken.

The next year they shot him dead in the dusty yard of his ranch house.

Tossing my saddle-bags to one side of the small upstairs hotel room I stretched out on the bed, hands behind my head. I stared at the pine-slat ceiling, watching the collected shadows and memories that imagination painted there. I was tired and angry and lonesome. I believed I could sleep.

They would not try to kill me before morning.

Dawn was harsh in its rising. The storm had broken and the glare of new sunlight was brilliant against the peaks of the snow-capped Rockies where the light struck first, making them appear like distant, bright golden beacons.

I hadn't slept much. All night the streets had been alive with the curses of brawling drunks, the sounds of breaking glass, and twice, gunshots until long after midnight. I stood looking out the window at the alley below me, littered with bottles, broken crates and garbage. A man slept huddled in the doorway of the harness shop opposite. The dream I had had for Stratton Valley when I first guided the new settlers in, a clean new town on a beautiful land, had long faded, the town itself turned into a nightmare hellhole.

Stratton was no better than the places most of the hopeful new people had left in the East. Worse, maybe, now that Peebles had moved in and declared himself king.

I rinsed off, dug a clean blue shirt from my roll, strapped on my Colt and went downstairs. The restaurant was across the lobby through swinging doors, and I strolled that way. The desk clerk – a different one – watched my passing with hawkish amusement.

It was early still, and the steamy interior of the restaurant was mostly silent except for the clinking of silver against plates, a few murmured conversations between scattered diners. Stratton was a late-rising town, as it would be after its long nightly revelries. I caught a flicker of notice in the tired eyes of an aproned, doughy waitress and seated myself at one of the small round tables covered with red-checked cloths. I took my hat off and placed it on one of the spare chairs. The waitress brought me a cup of coffee without having been asked. I nodded my thanks.

'What will it be this morning?' she asked, attempting a smile.

'Whatever's up,' I replied. 'As long as it's warm.'

'Hotcakes, eggs and ham?' she suggested.

'That'll do the job,' I answered. She shambled

11

away, scribbling the order down on a pad. My interest had already been drawn to the other end of the small restaurant. Even from the back, the young man clearing off one of the tables looked familiar and when he turned, a tray of dirty dishes in his hands, I saw that I had been right.

As the aproned man trudged past me I said, 'How's things, Toby?'

Toby Trammel glanced at me and nearly dropped the tray of dishes. He opened his mouth to speak but nothing came out for long moments.

'Tom,' he said at last, resting the tray on my table. 'Tom Quinn!'

'Unless I've got a double,' I said with a smile. Toby wiped his right hand on his apron and we shook. The uneasy, fair-haired man before me looked nothing like the cocky youngster I had last met. He seemed uncertain, glanced at the kitchen as if someone might scold him for pausing in his work. Toby Trammel had been one of the best young wranglers I had ever seen. Obviously embarrassed by his present circumstances, he turned his eyes down.

'Good to see you, Tom. Really.'

'I'd like to talk with you, Toby. When do you get off work?'

'I've been here since five. I generally get off by noon unless there's a real rush.'

'Let's say noon, then. I'm in room 10. Come up then.'

'Sure, Tom, I'd like that,' he answered, still looking around nervously. The waitress had emerged from the kitchen, and Toby, looking as frightened as a schoolboy, hefted the tray and hurried away.

Breakfast was hot, filling and well-made, but I couldn't enjoy it much. The hotel, the restaurant, the town had an ominous aspect, as if something heavy were about to collapse. Later, I went out onto the street and strolled down the plankwalks, studying Stratton. Broken windows, sun-faded paint, chipped sidings. When I had left, the town had been bustling with new merchants building their shops, with families shopping in the street, with cowhands from the outlands, tipping their hats to strolling ladies.

When I left there had been Mary Ford standing, watching as I rode out on my paint pony. . . .

I stood watching the town for a long while. Ne'er-do-wells, gunmen, whiskey-soaked men lounging on the corners, waiting for the saloons to open. A sycamore-tree I had planted in the plaza stood broken, neglected and sere. Beyond were the new redbrick buildings of a courthouse and jail, erected in my absence. I had no wish to see these symbols of Shelley Peebles's new kingdom.

I wandered back through the sad town, amazed that what I had built from nothing had come to such degeneration. I could just ride away, leave it to the barbarians, but I still felt a sense of obligation to the people of Stratton, a desire to avenge the desecration of the frontier promise I had offered them.

After cleaning and oiling my guns, I stretched out on my hotel bed and dozed a little while, waiting for Toby Trammel.

The knock on my door was timid, nevertheless I fisted one of my Colt revolvers before I answered it. Toby entered the room looking like a ghost of his former self. Always eager, brash and confident, he now looked ready to jump at his own shadow. He had been at my side on the way West and we had spent many nights around lonely camp-fires, drinking coffee and watching the long, starry skies. Now I hardly recognized him.

'Sit down, Toby,' I said, gesturing toward the single wooden chair in the room. I sat on the bed, placing my Colt on the scarred table next to it.

'Tom . . . it's so good to see you.' His voice faltered, and I realized then that it was shame that was causing his embarrassment.

'Want a job, Toby?' I asked without preliminaries.

'Real work?' he asked. An eager grin formed rapidly, rapidly fell away as questions gathered in his eyes.

'Real work, likely fighting work,' I said honestly. 'I intend to take Shelley Peebles down.'

'It can't be done!'

'Maybe not,' I admitted, 'but I think I can do it.'

'He has an army of men.'

'I know that,' I said and Toby's smile lingered a little longer now as he saw the intent in my eyes.

'You're crazy, you know,' he said.

'I've been told that before.'

I could see the uncertainty begin to build again in Toby's expression. I tried to give him a way out. I didn't want to Shanghai anyone into a game he didn't care to play. It was risky business I was talking about. No man weighs his own life lightly or wishes to sacrifice it to no end.

'I know I'm asking a lot. I'm promising nothing, Toby. Also,' I went on, 'I know you have steady work, a comfortable life. . . .'

'Oh, damn you, Tom!' Toby exploded as if he believed I was toying with him. He smiled apologetically, ran his hand over his pale, thinning hair and then wiped his hand on his chest as if he were still wearing an apron.

He took a deep breath and closed his eyes

briefly before going on. 'We were working for Tyler Holt – Barney Weber and me – and then they came and shot down Tyler because he refused to sell out his parcel to the Peebles syndicate, and the ranch folded. There was no work left in the valley for those who were on the wrong side of Peebles. We had no choice but to run or to take whatever job we could find.

'Barney and me, we didn't even have enough silver in our jeans to make a run. I went to work in the restaurant washing dishes because that was all I could find. Peebles comes in from time to time just to show me off as an example of what can happen to anyone who's tried to go up against him.'

'What happened to Barney?' I asked.

'He's mucking out the Tabor Stables at the far end of town,' Toby said, regaining some of his composure. 'We figure to try drifting out of the country together when we have enough cash to set ourselves up somewhere.'

'Do you think that Barney would want to work for me too?' I asked carefully. Beyond the window the Colorado skies had cleared. A few puffy clouds drifted slowly past, shadowing the long country in moving patches.

'Tom, are you serious about trying to shut down Peebles? About cleaning up this town? By yourself?'

I nodded again, returning my eyes to Toby. 'I built this town. I have the right to destroy it.'

'What would. . . ?' he hesitated. 'Have you talked to Mary?'

'I saw her. She seems to think I want to kill Ben and Will.'

'Do you?'

'Were they in on it? In on Tyler's murder?' I asked without answering his question.

'I don't know.' He shook his head. 'It was a crazy night with gunfire erupting everywhere across the range. Barney and I were riding night-watch on the herd. We had to choose between holding the cattle and leaving them to stampede or rushing to the main house to defend it.'

He said it miserably, and I considered that he must have suffered many nights of guilt over his decision to stay with the herd.

'It was your job, Toby,' I said.

'Yes, it was,' he said almost gratefully. 'Tom . . . I don't know what you have in mind, but I'm with you if you need me. I haven't the money to ride away, and what I'm doing now is killing whatever I have left of a soul.'

'What about Barney?' I asked.

'Do you want to talk to him?'

'I'd appreciate it if you would ask him, Toby. You two are long-time partners. Be honest with him. Explain how things are, let him know there's a huge risk involved.'

Toby rose, still looking uncertain. I asked him:

'You and Barney. You still have your six-guns and a couple of horses?'

'Yes,' Toby said with a returning grin. 'Those are the last things a man in this country would sell.' Then: 'Tom – you do have a plan, don't you? I mean. . . .'

'Yes, Toby, I do have a plan. But I can't promise you that it will be easy. Nothing is going to be easy from here on.'

TWO

It didn't take them long to come after me. I crossed the rutted main street of Stratton at the noon hour, and entered a shady alley behind Sturdevant's general store on my way to Hugh Sinclair's stable where I had put the gray horse I now rode up for the night. The alley was so narrow that I could have stuck out both arms and touched the sides of the buildings. It was deep in shadow and cool since the sun could not reach it. A dozen steps into the alley I heard boot-steps behind me and, before I could swivel around, two thick arms were thrown around me. From ahead a second man appeared, a confident smile on his thin lips, an axe-handle in his hands.

I threw an elbow back, causing the man holding me to grunt with surprise, then I stamped down hard on his instep with my boot-heel. He relaxed his grip a little and I was able to raise my arms inside his and break his grip.

The man with the axe-handle was strides away from me, his hickory club raised high. Instinct at times like those causes a man to try to duck, to run, but either is a bad choice. You go forward. I charged into the man with the club, throwing my shoulder against his chest. He couldn't lever the axe handle against my skull as he had intended once I was inside its arc. I kept my legs moving and drove him to the ground, swinging my fist into his jaw.

The first man was now rushing into the fight, wanting to help finish me off but I rolled away from the stunned man on the ground and slipped my walnut-gripped Colt from its holster. The ratcheting sound of the hammer being drawn back seemed loud even in the middle of the Stratton day.

Will Ford threw his thick arms skyward and halted in his tracks. Rushing a man with a club is one thing; I wouldn't recommend charging a cocked and loaded Colt .44.

Breathing heavily, I rose and stepped away from Ben Ford, kicking the axe-handle out of his grip. Sullenly Ben remained where he was. He wore no belt gun, I saw, nor did Will. 'Get up,' I told Ben heavily. 'Then both of you against the wall and tell me what this is about.'

'You came to kill us,' Will said in a high-pitched voice that did not match his bullish frame. 'What do you expect us to do?'

Ben was rubbing his jaw with the back of his hand. He glared at me silently from the shadows of the alley, his eyes murderous. I did not holster my gun, nor lower the hammer. I spoke evenly to Mary's two brothers, trying to make them understand.

'I didn't come here hunting you boys,' I told them.

'They told us. . . .' Ben said fiercely.

'Whoever told you that is lying, trying to get you to do their work for them. Can't you see that? We were trail-mates on the way West! We all took care of each other. I was planning on settling down with Mary! Has it been so long ago that you don't remember who Tom Quinn is?'

I turned away, sudden anger building within me. I slid my pistol into leather and muttered, 'The hell with you, then.' I picked up my hat and started on toward Sturdevant's, not bothering to cast them a backward glance.

The big gray with the splash of white on its chest seemed happy to see me. I have often wondered if horses, like dogs left alone, feel abandoned when their master goes away. I settled my bill with Sturdevant's stablehand, a kid of no more than fifteen who watched me with a sort of awe I could not explain. After saddling up, I rode my pony at a walk along the wash behind the town where the willow-trees were beginning their spring flourish, toward Tabor's stable where I was to meet Toby Trammel.

There were five stables in Stratton – not an unusual number even for such a small town. Every man owned a horse, the stagecoach used them, the freight wagons. Without horses there was no commerce possible, no transportation across the vast distances. The stables where a leg-weary, far-ridden horse could be cooled and provisioned were as vital to any town as any other institution.

I saw Toby before I reached Tabor's. Sitting behind the squat, weathered building he held the reins to his hammerhead sorrel – the same horse he had ridden West years before. He looked weary, uncertain, but at the sound of my gray's hoofbeats he brightened and rose to meet me.

'I was afraid you'd forgotten us,' he said. 'I quit my job. I've been wondering what's going to become of me.'

'So do we all,' I said, resting a hand on his shoulder. 'Have you talked to Barney?'

'Yes,' he said, drawing out the word doubtfully. 'But he wants to see you.' Toby shrugged. 'He isn't quite sure what to do either. He has a job here, you see, a bed in the loft every night. He's not sure what it is you have in mind, what his chances are.'

'I'm not either,' I said honestly. 'I am offering an opportunity for each of you boys to own a parcel of my own land – if we win. It's a gamble, yes, but tell Barney he has to weigh that against mucking out horse-stalls and sleeping in haylofts. I can't tell either one of you what to do. It's only an offer. I don't want anyone along who doesn't want to be there. If you don't want to ride with me, well . . . there's always other places that need dishwashers, other stables that need shoveling out.'

'I'll talk to Barney again,' Toby said with a smile reminiscent of the old Toby Trammel.

We trailed out northward at four in the afternoon. Me, Toby Trammel and Barney Weber, who looked now like a man who had shed his doubts and felt liberated: a prisoner who has received an unexpected reprieve. The spirits of the two seemed to lighten as we rode, their shackles undone. The long valley, thick with grass, studded here and there with black-eyed susans and blue lupine, was crossed by silver rills and dotted with bright, sunlit ponds. Above it all the purple

Rockies with their snowcaps brooded over the pleasing land. With every mile Toby and the freckle-faced Barney Weber seemed to be regaining their youthful vigor and joy.

I just hoped I would prove worthy of their blind trust. I had doubts, but I didn't speak of them on the trail. I listened to the whish of the gray's hoofs through the long grass, watched as the two younger men joked and laughed, and kept to myself my private thoughts.

Too many of which concerned Mary Ford.

We began to pass small herds of cattle fattening on the lush grass. Most of them were longhorns, but we could see dozens of white-faced Herefords among them. Peebles, whatever he was, was not a fool. The day of the longhorn steer was passing and he had begun bringing in the fatter, more choice breed.

The problem was, the cattle were on my land.

I had explained matters to Barney and Toby Trammel as we progressed northward on that sunny day, the rich scent of new grass in our nostrils.

'As you boys remember, Stratton Valley was first staked out by Gil Stratton in the late '60s. It was virtually worthless, being so far from civilization, nothing but raw land, and Gil himself had trouble making a living off it. He was a trapper and that was all he knew. There's plentiful timber, but what was there to do with it? Freight it out? To where?

'Me,' I continued, 'I ran into Gil in the '70s when he was already old, bent and tired of the wilderness life. I guess he liked me some. I was drifting aimlessly, and we wintered up together. I was the son he never had, I suppose, and I was fond of the old man. When he passed, I found out that he had willed me his property, that is two hundred and twenty thousand acres of Colorado meadowland.

'Still,' I told them, 'that hardly made me a wealthy man. Land was cheap in those times. I had no prospects of finding ore like they had down in Denver or Leadville. Cattle weren't run in Colorado in those days, winters being what they are, there was no way to bring in hay after the first snows fell. There was still the timber, but no way to harvest it or transport it – besides, I never wished to destroy the beauty of the high country by cutting the forests.'

'Is that when you went East?' Barney Weber asked.

I nodded 'I was still a drifter at heart, I suppose. I wanted to see St Louis. What I found was a group of pilgrims who wanted to find new homes in the West, but were at a loss as to know where to settle.'

'So you led them here.'

'Yes.'

If it had not been for Mary Ford's bright eyes I might never have considered it, but. . . .

'Honestly, Mr Quinn,' the young lady had said as we walked out one night away from the dully glowing camp-fires of their wagon encampment on the outskirts of St Louis, 'we don't know what to do. Mr Tyler Holt says it's still a thousand miles to the Oregon country, and my mother is ill. Father is not an experienced trailsman either. It seems like this rambling will go on forever and is doomed to failure.'

That was the first time I had met Mary. Determined to help her, I had met with Tyler Holt, a weary, well-meaning man in over his head in the vastness of the West, and offered him a proposition.

'I know a place where there is room enough for all of you to build a home. A place you can put down roots and raise your families. If you will trust me to guide you.'

Gil Stratton would have wanted it that way.

'I can't believe you just gave it all away,' Toby Trammel said, waving a hand around him, indicating the deep blue stands of spruce, the long-grass valleys, the silver rills.

'Maybe there's some Indian in me,' I answered.

'You know that they believe no man can ever own the land he travels. You do what you can to help people.' Unfortunately, I had not helped anyone much. Now Shelley Peebles had built a cattle empire on the land and the good families had been ruined or driven off or burned out.

'So, how do you figure to. . . ?' Toby asked as we continued our plodding way northward, leading a pack mule carrying hastily purchased provisions.

'How do I figure to *try?*'

Our horses startled a covey of partridge, and I briefly watched them fly away on bright wings. 'Boys, I am some dumb but not plumb dumb. When I deeded the Stratton sections over to the settlers I retained the upper ten thousand acres for myself. Gill Stratton's original cabin and the Pocono headwaters. I was saving it for. . . .'

For Mary and me to live on.

'That gives me the upper hand,' I explained to them.

'I don't see what you mean, Tom,' Barney Weber said.

'I think I do,' Toby said. 'You mean to cut off the town's water supply, don't you, Tom?'

I only nodded. He had it right.

'But that's crazy!' Barney said, his face flushing deeply enough to hide his freckles. 'It's a wild plan! Even if it could be done, it would surely lead

27

to an all-out shooting war.'

'Right three times, Barney,' I answered. 'If you boys want to turn around now, I won't hold it against you.' They only glanced at each other and smiled. Toby said:

'I guess we'll stick, Tom. It'll sure be something to see!'

We continued to pass cattle, fat and sleek in the long grass. We halted at the head of the cut-off through Gunnison. Notch. The wind had freshened. It shifted the tails and manes of our ponies. The pines swayed in peaceful unison on the fringes of the long valley.

Toby had removed his hat to wipe his forehead with his red bandanna. 'It occurs to me,' he said, 'that we passed your boundary marker about a half a mile back. Peebles's cattle are on your land, Tom.'

'They won't be for long,' I replied. 'Boys, I am going to take the cut-off.'

'Going to see Mrs. Holt?' Barney Weber asked.

'Yes. It's an obligation. I have to see how she is doing, if she needs anything. It can't be easy for her running that place with Tyler dead.' They nodded in understanding. 'I want you two to ride ahead to Gil Stratton's old place, the stone cabin – you know it, don't you, Toby? We'll be staying there for a while.

'I'd like you to look around, sweep the place out, check for packrats, any signs of owl-nests in the chimney, generally clean up, mow down any weeds that might have sprung up in the yard. Chop some firewood – just generally clean up and make yourselves useful.'

'What if some of the Peebles gang comes around?' Barney asked with some concern.

'Try to avoid any shooting incident. You can tell them the truth: that I just hired you to clean up. That's all you know. It goes without saying,' I added grimly, 'that you have the right to protect yourselves. If you need to fort up in that stone house, it would take an army to get you out of it. Old Gil constructed it to withstand Indian attacks, and he did it well. I'll be back as soon as I can make it.'

I watched the two men ride on. I knew they carried some concerns with them, but also I could tell from their expressions that they were pleased to be out in the open county once again, free men. I turned the big gray horse I rode toward the Gunnison cut-off, riding toward the ranch of Tyler Holt's widow and fatherless children.

I watched the long skies with their puffball clouds, the mountain peaks and deep forest with the pleasure of a returning prodigal, but I also kept my eyes open for any outriders. Most likely

29

none of Peebles's crew knew me by sight, nor could they have an idea of my intentions, but by now some word of the return of Tom Quinn must have reached Shelley Peebles's ears and he might have sent out riders to tell his men to watch for me, discourage me – or worse.

I cleared the east end of the pass and dropped through a stand of dark pines, startling a covey of mountain quail, hearing the chattering of silver squirrels in the tall trees. When I broke from the forest I saw the little, low-roofed log cabin Tyler Holt had built for his family, promising that in time it would be a home to be proud of. Once his first crop came in.

It didn't look now as if that crop had ever arrived. The ground was barren and dry. I could see where there had once been long furrows carved by Tyler's dawn-to-dusk labors. I saw no cattle, no horses, nothing but a few chickens scratching at the earth before the house, and these scattered at my arrival. I called to the house before swinging down.

'Hello! Anyone to home? Sadie? It's Tom Quinn!'

The door opened with the silence of uneasiness and the slow caution of fear.

'Tom?' an old woman's voice enquired with disbelief from the darkness of the log house's interior. 'Tom Quinn!'

'It's me, Sadie,' I assured her, and as I swung down from the gray horse's back, the door was flung wide and Sadie Holt's broad, honest face appeared. She hoisted her dark, heavy skirts and stepped out onto the buckled porch, her fearful eyes brightening. I looped my horse's reins around the hitch rail and stepped up onto the porch, removing my hat before I spread my arms and walked to her, embracing the good-hearted old soul. For a moment we looked into each other's eyes. I saw kindness, fear, sorrow and the inroads of age in hers. What she saw in mine, I couldn't guess. She dabbed at her eyes with her apron.

'Come in, Tom. Do come in! You've been long on the trail. Let me fix you something to eat, boil some coffee.'

My stomach was growling, but I considered that the family had little enough to feed itself. 'I couldn't eat. Coffee sounds fine, Sadie.'

'Randall and George aren't here. They're out hunting game. But Julia is here. I'll get her. Sit down, Tom, sit down.'

I did, seating myself at the roughly made puncheon table while Sadie called for her eldest child, Julia. I felt, rather than saw, the poverty shadowing the house. I could guess that the cupboards were almost bare, and that they had simply been living off the land as best they could.

After a minute Sadie returned, tugging at the hand of her daughter. Julia had blossomed into young womanhood since the days we had ridden West. Her reddish hair was worn loose, her eyes downcast. She had a tragic sense of hopelessness about her.

'Julia, you may not remember Tom Quinn,' Sadie said.

'I remember him,' the girl answered, with her eyes still cast down. 'Nice to see you again, Mr Quinn. Mother, I have to finish the laundry.'

'Wouldn't you like to visit with Tom for awhile?'

'If she has work to do, she'd better finish it,' I said hastily. I had the idea that Julia did not wish to visit with me. Natural shyness or some undefined grudge against the man who had led her family here, I couldn't say. I smiled at her, and she nodded and scurried away. Sadie looked disappointed in her daughter.

'How about that coffee?' I asked to break Sadie's train of thought.

'Surely. The fire's already built – for supper.'

As she bustled around the cramped, dark kitchen I asked her about herself, the ranch, Tyler's death.

'When the Peebles men shot Tyler down I wept

for a week,' Sadie said, her broad back to me. 'Then I got angry. I was so angry I wanted to take up a shotgun myself and go after him. The boys had to stop me. I was hysterical, Tom. Then I sat down and started crying some more.

'The way it happened was that one night a group of riders appeared just before midnight. They carried torches.. Our stock was driven off, the fields intentionally trampled by the herd, and then set ablaze. I stopped Randall and George from going out into the darkness with their guns. I knew what would happen.'

'It's a wonder they let the house remain standing,' I commented.

'They weren't going to, Tom, but one of the riders, a man named Kit Stacy, shouted out that he would shoot any man who set fire to a house with women and children in it. At least one of them had that much pity.'

Sadie returned to the table with two heavy ceramic cups and a speckled blue coffee-pot. She poured us each half a cup and seated herself with a sigh, jabbing at her gray-streaked hair with agitated fingers so that a few hair pins slipped free and a strand fell across her forehead.

'They left us the cabin, but no stock, not so much as a mule to plow the fields.'

She shook off the unhappy memories. Her

attempted smile was weary but very real. 'So tell me, Tom, where in the world have you been? What have you been doing all this time?'

Sipping at the scalding coffee, I told her slowly where I had been since Mary Ford had broken our engagement.

'I found work as line scout for the Colorado and Eastern Railroad. It was my job to find the best route for the new line, and sometimes to negotiate with the Indians. I was the first one in, followed by the surveyors, and finally the steel crews, mostly Irishmen. Later I stayed on, working with the surveyors and learned a little about that. I took whatever work the railroad would offer me. I learned to be a powder-man – that is, to use explosives to clear the way through hard rock. I swung a sledge-hammer for a while as well.

'A representative from Denver told me that I had enough experience to supervise a crew and they might even consider moving me to an office job.'

'Impressive!'

'I suppose. But can you see Tom Quinn in an office in Denver, shuffling papers? Besides. . . .'

'Besides, you were still thinking about Mary Ford.'

I winced, then smiled. 'You are a wise woman, Sadie Holt. I had more money banked than I'd ever had. A year of not paying for a roof over my head, for food, horses – all of that was covered by the railroad – had left me pretty well fixed. I was still thinking I might be able to get Mary to change her mind.'

'To bribe her into marrying you, you mean?'

'That never works, does it,' I said darkly. 'But I think I knew that anyway. It was finding an article in the newspaper about a range war in Stratton that brought me back. There was a list of people who had been shot by unknown assailants. One of them was Tyler Holt.'

'My husband was never involved in a range war. It was murder, Tom.'

'I know that, Sadie. That's why I'm here.'

'There's nothing that can be done, Tom,' she said with urgency. Her blue-veined hands reached across the table and briefly covered mine. 'Don't try it! There's too many of them. Nothing is worth your life. Don't stir things up again. For your own sake.'

'It's a little too late, Sadie,' I told her with a crooked smile. 'I've already started the ball rolling.'

We stood on the porch for awhile, the low sun scattering burnt-orange and crimson streamers across the sky. I watched a flight of doves winging for home, heard distantly the howl of a mountain wolf.

I was up into the saddle, had half-turned the big gray horse homeward before I asked:

'Were Ben and Will Ford here that night? The night Tyler was killed?'

'I don't know, Tom,' Sadie said with soft sadness. 'I just don't know. It was midnight. Most of them wore masks. I just don't know.'

I touched the brim of my hat and rode away. For a brief moment I caught a glimpse of Julia Holt in the open doorway, hands clasped, watching after me. I had no idea what her memories of me were, what unintended sins I might have committed by bringing the Holt family here to the unhappy fringe of civilization. Neither of these lonely women had the spirit left to fight their sadness.

I did hope that Julia would be the one to find the twenty-dollar gold piece I had left on the table under my saucer knowing that Sadie, out of pride, would run out into the yard, calling after me.

At the moment, as dusk purpled the sky and I returned to the cut-off, I forced myself to banish these concerns from my mind and concentrate on what I had come back to Stratton to accomplish: ruin Shelley Peebles and destroy the hell-town he had erected over lost dreams.

THREE

There was a faint, oddly comforting glow showing in the slit windows of old Gil Stratton's stone house – my house. I could smell woodsmoke and sourdough biscuits. The yard was rough and dry, but clear of weeds. The boys, I thought, had done a remarkable amount of work in a short time.

I hailed the house before riding in. True, it was my house, but I knew Barney and Toby Trammel would be inside with nervous trigger fingers, expecting anything on our first night in the long valley. The smoke from the chimney would tip off any roaming Peebles rider that someone was encroaching on what they perceived to be their range.

I swung down, loosened the cinches on the big gray horse and stamped into the house, the boys having opened it wide for me.

'We've got the stable mostly cleared out,'

Barney Weber said, and offered: 'Want me to put your horse up for you?'

I nodded my appreciation and looked around the stone cabin, finding it swept and as neat as could be expected after a year of disuse. There were no curtains and such. Neither Gil Stratton nor I had ever had a woman around to worry about trifles. Nevertheless, this was a fine homecoming. The woven leather-bottomed chair fit me just right and Toby had brought me a mug of coffee. He sat opposite me on one of the stiff wooden chairs surrounding the table, without asking questions, but I knew what was on his mind – what were we going to do next?

'Tomorrow,' I told them after Barney had returned from putting my horse up, 'I'd like you boys to mow what hay you can. Stack it in the stable. I don't want the ponies grazing out in the open.'

They nodded their understanding. We didn't want our mounts shot or stolen by raiding Peebles gang riders. I went on. 'It might be a slow process, because I think it's best if one of you scythed while the other stood watch in the pines with a rifle at the ready, I have no idea what this mob might consider doing once they realize that I'm here to stay.'

'You won't be here, Tom?' Toby Trammel

asked, frowning slightly.

'No. I have to go into Stratton, to the freight office. I'm expecting a shipment. I'll take the mule along to haul it.'

'We have plenty of supplies,' Barney said, his freckled face puzzled.

'This is something else, Barney. Something I've had planned since before I rode back in.'

Neither man made a comment, or so much as blinked. They had confidence in me. I only hoped it wasn't misplaced trust. I thought about laying out my plan for them, but did not. There would be time to warn them later. What I had in mind was going to raise hell in the big valley. I was going to war not only against Peebles, but his entire, rat-infested town.

I lay awake long after midnight, thinking mostly of Mary Ford. I couldn't help myself. I slept fitfully until just after false dawn had grayed the eastern skies, and then realized that my dream had continued until Mary's beautiful face had altered, becoming the young fearful-eyed Julia Holt's. I swore at myself as I rose in the silence of the morning. A man can be such a fool.

The night-birds were still singing as I trailed out of the stone cabin's yard, leading the pack mule. I frightened off a small herd of deer that had been peacefully grazing among the cattle. Silently I apologized to them; I had not meant to disturb their breakfasting.

When I would approach cattle quietly feeding on the dew jeweled long grass I would silently hie them before me, drifting them south. The dumb animals had no idea why I was doing it, but a few would lift up confused bovine heads and lope away toward the south. I had nothing against these animals either, but their owner had chosen the wrong land to graze them on. This was my land, my grass, my water, and though I did not begrudge it to any animal, none of it could be taken over by Shelley Peebles for his own gain.

He was, simply, a murderer, a thief and a pirate.

The sun was full in my eyes when I turned toward the town of Stratton. The land here was grassy knolls, a bit of trickling rill, scattered pines and a few white-oak trees. I never heard the first gunshot until I saw lead explode into the leather of my pommel. Then the rolling thunder of a long gun echoed down the valley. Instantly I went low across the withers of my gray, who, startled already, leaped into a run at my urging. The confused pack-mule followed us blindly as we raced for the shelter of the pine-woods.

That shot had been no accident, no warning bullet. It had been intended to kill. The marksman had missed his intended target only by inches. There were other guns firing – some from the forest, some from a distant site I could not determine as I raced headlong into the pines, slowing my mount only to keep him from crashing recklessly into the trees.

I swung down, unsheathed my Winchester '73 and went to my belly, watching the long valley for signs of movement while I kept an ear open for any sounds behind me. Nothing but the tips of the cool pines moved. Distantly a crow cawed; the gray horse, circling impatiently, pawed at the ground. But there were no other sounds in the silent mountain valley.

Someone called out and my fingers twitched on the lever of my long-gun.

'Don't shoot, Tom!' a familiar voice called out.

I didn't relax, but got to one knee in a ready firing position.

'Did you hear me, Tom?'

'I did! Come ahead with empty hands.'

From the deep shadows of the blue woods Ben and Will Ford emerged, both with their hands held high so that I could see they were carrying no weapons. I rose unsteadily, my rifle at belt-level.

'What is it?' I growled at Mary's brothers, the hammer on my Winchester still drawn back, my finger still curled around the cold trigger.

'It wasn't us, Tom,' Will Ford said, his thick body stiff with emotion. 'We were coming out to talk to you . . . to apologize, actually. We saw some men across the creek in the boulders. They started to shoot at you, and, well . . . we fired back.'

'It's true,' Ben Ford said. 'Tom, would we have come in if we wanted to kill you?'

'No,' I had to admit, 'I suppose not. I guess I owe you boys an apology, too.'

'We had a talk with Mary last night,' big Will Ford said, crouching down on his heels. 'She told us that you promised her that you wouldn't hunt us down.'

That wasn't exactly what I had said, but I let it pass. Ben Ford went on quickly:

'We were never out at the Holt place the night Tyler was killed, Tom. Honest! Our family lost its holdings, too. Land you had given to us. Me and Ben, we've been up half the night thinking things through, and well – we couldn't have been more wrong than we were jumping you back in town.'

'We were scared,' Will Ford, so big that you'd think he could never be scared of anything, added.

'Do you mind telling me why you boys just didn't drift away after all the trouble started?' I had dusted off my jeans and gathered up the reins to my gray horse and those of the doleful mule. 'Most people did.'

'It's kind of shameful,' Ben Ford said, his face shy and distant in the dappled shade. 'And you might not want to hear it.'

'Well?' I prompted. His bearish brother answered.

'We got to keep a little of the land we had left,' Big Will said, 'so long as we didn't go up against Peebles, Kit Stacy and that bunch.'

'And you agreed?'

'That's the part that's shameful, Tom. Yes, we agreed. Ten acres beats the hard road.'

'Tell him the rest of it, Will,' Ben prompted. The big man couldn't look me in the eye. Somehow, I already knew what he was going to say. Still, it was punishing when he did.

'Shelley Peebles wants Mary. So long as he has that hope . . .' he shrugged heavily, 'we have the little bit of land that is ours.'

It took me a while to digest what they were saying to me. A man goes away for a year and so much can change. I read all sorts of innuendo into what they were telling me, not telling me. In the end, I only replied, 'I see,' even though I could see where their shame was coming from.

'Now what?' I asked with resurrected strength

as I swung aboard my horse.

'Tom . . .' the brothers glanced at each other, 'we were hoping you might tell *us*.'

'Do you want jobs?' I asked without irony. 'I can't promise much in wages, but there could be a lot in the way of satisfaction.'

'You're going to take him on, aren't you? Peebles, I mean,' Will asked with a smile creasing his broad face.

'Yes,' I answered simply.

'He's got a dozen gunslingers,' Ben said worriedly.

'Yes, I know. Do you want jobs or not?'

Big Will spoke for both of them. 'I guess we're both pretty tired of being who we have been, Tom. If you'll have us, I guess we'll go along for the ride.'

I got my first look at Shelley Peebles in Stratton that sun-drenched morning. I had expected a man larger than life, wide-shouldered as a bear, mean-eyed and dangerous-looking. He was none of those. He was mild-looking with a thin mustache and a small revolver riding high on his hip beneath the skirts of a tailored gray suit. He could have been a banker or a minor public functionary. I had to remind myself that this was the man who had orchestrated the death of Tyler

44

Holt, driven away dozens of young settlers and likely planned to have me killed in the long valley earlier that day.

He watched with seeming indifference as the Ford brothers and I picked up the goods I had ordered weeks ago from the freight office and strapped them onto the unprotesting, brown-eyed mule.

Only once did our eyes lock across the rutted street. I liked none of what I saw in his stare. The man wanted me dead. Was it his lust for Mary, the land, the challenge to his authority that burned in those eyes? All of these, I guessed. No matter – a war had begun. The first pawns had been offered. My advantage was that, at the moment, he could not know what my next move might be.

'Anything else, Tom?' big Will Ford asked as he strapped down the mule's burden.

'Yes. Ammunition, and plenty of it.'

It was already late afternoon before we returned to the valley. The Fords and I had paused to have breakfast. It was there that Ben pointed out the Missouri gunfighter, Kit Stacy. The blond man in fringed buckskins with guileless blue eyes, not more than twenty years old, at a guess, sat watching his steaming coffee-cup dreamily as if he had not a worry in the world.

'Don't let his looks fool you,' Will muttered. 'A sneeze will pop that Colt from his holster.'

I nodded without answering, drinking my own coffee.

Sadie Holt had told me that the gunman had prevented the Peebles night-riders from burning down her home. That proved nothing except that the man from Missouri had some sort of conscience. I couldn't expect him to give me the same sort of consideration. Not if what I had heard about him was the truth.

As night fell and the peaceful sounds of the larks in the pines announced the end of day, I began to lay out my plan for the men gathered. Toby Trammel and Barney sat nearest to the fire. Big Will Ford had taken the other leather-bottomed chair, leaving Ben Ford to seat himself on the Indian rug in the corner of the stone house. We were running out of chairs! But I'd rather have that happen than to run out of fighting men.

'In the morning. . . .' I began, and got no further as Toby Trammel, quick and alert as an Apache, put his finger to his lips and crossed to the horizontal slit window.

'Someone's coming,' Toby whispered.

Every man reached for his weapons.

'Can you tell who it is?' Big Will Ford asked.

'No!' Toby hissed. 'See if they hail the house. Otherwise they're up to no good.'

I myself had the walnut grips of my Colt in hand and my finger against the cold blue steel of the trigger. Crouched low, I waited. A voice sang out:

'Tom! Hello! It's Randall and George Holt here. Can we come forward?'

With relief, a little shakily if I have to admit it, I holstered my revolver and opened the door to greet Tyler Holt's sons.

'Come on in, boys,' I said.

Both boys, each with determined but shy faces, tramped into the room. For a moment there was a heavy indecisiveness in the air as the groups confronted each other. It was especially palpable when the sons of Tyler Holt looked into the eyes of the Ford brothers, who had been implicated in the night-raid that had killed their father. I tried my best to defuse the situation.

'Find a seat, boys, wherever you can. We're all here for the same purpose – to take down Shelley Peebles and his mob.'

'As you were saying, Tom,' Toby Trammel said, helping me along, though the awkwardness continued to hang heavy in the room.

'Just a minute,' I said lifting a hand. I studied the faces of Tyler Holt's young sons. 'Do you boys know what is at stake here? What could happen to any of you?'

'Our mother told us that you were going to kick Shelley Peebles out of his britches. That's why we're here, with her blessing, Tom. How could we do less? The man killed our father.'

I didn't like the idea of Sadie and young Julia being left alone across the notch, but I only nodded my head, grateful for the young men's support which might very well be needed – and resumed.

'I don't know if any of you boys noticed what I packed in from the freight office today. If not, I'll tell you right now. It was dynamite.'

There was a brief, puzzled pause as they glanced at each other. I went on. 'I'm going to blow up the Pocono River headwaters and drive Peebles and his land barons out of this territory.'

FOUR

'You're crazy, Tom!' big Will Ford said.

'Likely,' I agreed, 'but that's what I'm going to do – cut off the water to the entire range and the town of Stratton itself.'

'But you can't. . . .' Randall Holt began.

'Sure I can,' I said almost cheerfully. 'I've got the dynamite. As some of you know, I worked for the railroad for months clearing roadbeds, and I haven't forgotten my training.'

'Tom!' Toby said, now looking fearful as he half-rose from the Indian blanket he had been sitting on. 'Peebles will come looking for blood. Beyond that, you haven't a legal leg to stand on!'

'Do I not?' I countered. 'I hold the water rights to the Pocono Basin, Toby. It's my understanding that I can do what I like with the river. If they contend that I'm wrong, they can let the courts sort through it. Even with Peebles's hand-picked judge in place it will take years to adjudicate. Myself, I have the time – but there will be a lot of thirsty steers and a lot of dry people in Stratton.

'I'm taking this valley back for the people who worked for it,' I said, growing more intensely angry than I had meant to. 'If any one of you wishes to leave, he is free to go out that door. You're in for a war, men, if you stick with me. Otherwise – no hard feelings, no regrets. I hope our trails cross again somewhere down the line.'

Not a man rose to leave.

'All right,' I said. 'Come morning we are going to raise some hell! Check and load every weapon you have, because this will not come easy.'

I was up with the dawn. Barney Weber had been up even earlier and started the coffee boiling on the stove. I poured a cup from the gallon pot, stepped out onto the porch and watched the new sun flush the high snow-capped peaks. There was a frost on the long grass and a chill breeze stirring. I saw Barney across the yard, returning from the stable. There was a worried look in the freckle-faced kid's eyes. He stamped up onto the porch to stand beside me for a minute.

'Couldn't sleep?' I asked.

'Not a minute. I started the coffee and went out to look in on the horses.'

'I thank you for both,' I told him. The pine-trees were beginning to sway in the stiffening wind that always rose with the dawn up here. I glanced again at Barney's nervous eyes and then turned my gaze away toward the vast distances.

I told him quietly, 'Barney, what I said last night still goes. Any man who wants to leave can. Without any questions. Without condemnation.'

He hesitated a long time before he answered, our eyes still distant from each other's. 'It's just . . . Tom, men are going to die up here.'

'Likely.'

'Maybe a lot of men. I don't want to be one of them.'

'Nor do I, Barney.' I did meet his eyes directly now and said, 'I told you why I was going to fight this out. That doesn't mean you have to. You can ride out now, leave before any of the others are awake, with no shame attached to it – if you have a mind to.'

I wondered if that was not why he had been out in the stable, saddling his pony, hoping to slip away while we were still asleep. 'I'm kinda frightened, Tom,' he murmured.

'So am I,' I admitted. 'Every man makes his own choices. You do what you think is right.'

Again the wind gusted coldly. There were clouds massing in the high canyons and I wondered if it would rain again. My coffee had grown cold before I reached the bottom of my cup. I waited for Barney to tell me what he wanted to do. The *truth* of it.

'I believe I'll be staying, Tom. Let's have another cup of coffee, shall we?'

Inside I found the boys, sleepy-eyed and rumpled, settling in around the puncheon table. I waited for them to have coffee themselves and get their heads on before I handed out instructions.

'Toby, I want you to go with me this morning. We'll be riding into the Pocono Gorge. Ben, Will – you and George can ride the perimeter to the south. Watch for trouble, but push any Peebles beef you come across as far off my range as you can.

'Barney,' I said with no mention of his earlier timidity, 'you and young Randall Holt here stay around the house. Sort out the provisions, clean up whatever still needs to be cleaned. Keep alert. Fort up if anyone besides any of our crew rides in. Everyone clear on what his job is?'

Heads nodded. Only Toby looked doubtful. He had never been near to an explosion the size of the one he was going to see. He looked at my face, saw grim determination and shrugged. The boys began stamping into their boots, slinging their gunbelts on and shouldering into their winter coats.

Toby Trammel and I traced a trail through the cold pines, Toby leading the laden mule. The land went upward and only upward here as we paralleled the swiftly running Pocono River, the source of all the creeks and meandering rills that watered the long grass valley below us. Ahead, rising up 500 feet along the slopes of the gap known as the Crag, stood two broken granite spires that Gil Stratton had named the Sentinels, for obvious reasons. They stood beside the white-flowing, roaring river where it raced through the narrow gorge before it broke free of the channel and slowly spread itself out into peaceful, glittering streams.

'What are you meaning to do, Tom?' Toby asked with habitual trepidation. 'I mean . . . the dynamite?'

'I'm going to bring down the Sentinels, Toby. They're mine. The headwaters are mine. I'm going to form myself a nice deep lake.'

He looked up doubtfully at the jutting granite monoliths. 'It can't be done, Tom, can it?'

'It can be,' I assured him. 'This isn't something I thought up overnight. I know this land better than any man except Gil Stratton. I've come back with the skills the powder-men in the railroad crews taught me. I can bring the whole mountainside down, if I choose.

'And I choose,' I added grimly.

I heard Toby curse between clenched teeth. He liked none of this, but if ever a man rode with more raw determination than I was carrying with me on that day, I had not met him. Toby saw that and continued to follow along, shaking his head.

'Once we've set the charges, Toby, you can ride out of here. Rock will be flying, as you can imagine.'

'Tom,' Toby said, recovering his bold grin, 'I wouldn't miss this for the world. Though I still think you're crazy!'

'That seems to be the general consensus,' I agreed.

It was the work of an entire morning, setting the bundles of dynamite. Even with my practiced eye I wasn't sure I had gotten the charges in exactly the right position. I wished I had the long-honed skills of those men I had worked with on the Colorado & Eastern who thought nothing of blowing away entire mountainsides to force a path through for the westward-driving Iron Horse. But I thought I had learned enough in working for the railroad to drop the Sentinels and accomplish my goal.

Not until the early hours of afternoon had we planted the fuses, strung out what seemed to be miles of wire and settled ourselves in behind a huge stack of boulders on the back side of a piney slope. Earlier I had sent Toby off to picket the horses and the mule even further down the slope. Still they might bolt and run, but at least they would be safe.

'You don't have to stay here, Toby,' I said, giving him one last chance before I hit the detonator.

'Hell, Tom,' he said, crouching beside me. 'I've done my work – let me see the show!'

I wondered if he knew what he was in for. I did, having witnessed dozens of hard-rock blasts, but I just told him. 'Watch yourself,' and dropped the plunger on the detonating device.

At first there was only a small flicker of flame visible against the bases of the distant granite spires. Red and yellow, briefly touching eerie light to the stone monuments. Toby half-rose and peered that way. 'What went wrong, Tom?'

'Get down!' I shouted, grabbing him by the shoulder, for I knew the way of the fuses and that was their signal that all was well and that hell was about to break loose. No sooner had I spoken than the big, earth-shifting rumble of the dynamite packs exploding began. Toby hit the earth, his fingers in his ears.

There was no flame now, but the explosions,

one after the other, threw dust and boulders, fragments of the monoliths skyward. And they began to rain down on us, far away from the blasts though we were. The ground trembled beneath us and Toby rose again, fearfully, but not willing to miss what was to come next.

For a moment there was no sound, nothing but the settling of smaller fragments of stone around us. The heavy clouds of rock dust continued to blur our vision. Toby again looked at me with uncertainty, and I began to have doubts myself about how well I had learned my lessons of destruction.

Then, distantly, a creaking began, as if some behemoth were opening his dungeon door and I thought I saw – did see – the northern Sentinel sway ever so slightly. As Toby stepped beside me to watch, mouth agape, eyes scoured with dust, the northern monolith began to crumble at its base and the 500-foot spire slowly, inexorably began to tilt toward its twin. An odd creaking sound, grating and as loud as a dozen locomotives, followed as first one and then the other Sentinel collapsed earthward and the ground trembled again, angrily.

We pressed faces and bodies to the earth behind the boulders and stayed there until the last rumbling had settled to shuddering silence.

There was no sound in the forest when we rose, not a single bird or creature moved.

'Let's see what we've accomplished,' I said, dusting myself off with my hat. Our faces were dark with granite dust. My legs trembled slightly as we walked up the shale-strewn slope to view the destruction we had caused. Standing on a rocky shelf high above the gorge with the wind snatching at our clothes I could see that my execution of the Sentinels had been nearly perfect. Behind the newly formed stone dam the waters of the Pocono were beginning to back up, to swirl as if in frustration, to slow and spread out, forming a broad lake.

'God, Tom!' Toby Trammel said in awe. He removed his hat and wiped back his stringy blond hair. 'I wasn't sure you could do it.'

'Neither was I,' I answered, smiling at him as I watched the silver lake widen and capture the afternoon sunlight.

'But I was right,' Toby said distantly. 'I wouldn't have missed it for the world.'

As we rode southward once again, Toby commented, 'They'll have heard the blast all the way to Stratton.'

'Very likely.'

'They won't be able to guess what it was, but when the creeks start drying up and the town has no water, they'll come looking.'

'That's right, Toby.'

'With all of the gunmen Peebles can muster.'

I glanced at him from out of the shadow of my hat-brim. I remembered what I had told Barney Weber that morning and I repeated it to Toby Trammel. 'If you want to ride out now, Toby, it's all right.' But the wrangler only grinned at me and said:

'Tom, I wouldn't miss it for the world!'

There seemed to have been no trouble on the spread when Toby and I trailed in from The Crag. But both Randall Holt, rake in his hands and Barney Weber who was standing on the porch with a broom, stopped what they were doing and considered our streaked faces and dusty clothes with unvoiced questions. As we swung down from our horses, Barney asked as last:

'What in *hell* did you do up there, Tom! The explosion nearly knocked me off my feet.'

Sitting on the porch, my hat tilted back, I told them succinctly what we had done and reminded them, as if they hadn't already realized it, that I had definitely opened Pandora's box. Trouble would certainly be on its way.

Our own water supply was not going to be interrupted. Gil Stratton and I had spent many weeks digging a deep well behind the house. I rolled up my shirtsleeves and rinsed myself off with cold water drawn from its depths and then asked Toby:

'Is there still a print shop in Stratton?'

'Well, sure,' he said with puzzlement. I was getting used to my men looking at me in that way – as if they thought that I might be mad. Maybe I was, I don't know. 'We still have that one-sheet newspaper,' he told me, 'the Stratton *Gazette*. But old man Savage is gone now. He was forced out after he printed a few items that Shelley Peebles didn't care for. Do you mind if I ask what it is that you're up to now, Tom?'

I rolled my cuffs down, wiped my fingers through my damp hair and answered, 'Why, I think it's only right to give Shelley Peebles fair warning, Toby.'

'I don't think I get you, Tom,' Toby said, shaking his head worriedly.

I placed my hand briefly on his shoulder and said. 'You will.'

Toby and I cinched up again and started south to ride the ten miles to Stratton. The skies held clear except for a few high white clouds, but we could hear grumbling in the high mountains as thunder built menacingly.

Half a mile on we came upon Big Will Ford and George Holt riding toward us. We pulled up in a group and Will explained: 'We decided among us that two of us would ride back to the house and have dinner then spell the others while they did the same. Is that all right with you, Tom?'

'A man has to eat,' was all I said. At their curious looks, I went on to explain that Toby and I were riding into Stratton. Will's broad face lowered into a frown.

'Tom, Shelley Peebles will surely be out for your hide after what you've done today. Do you want us to ride with you?'

'He doesn't know yet what has happened. All he knows is that I'm back – Mary will have told him. Besides,' I added ruefully, 'he doesn't feel threatened by me. To him I'm of no more importance than a fly he has to shoo away. You boys get your dinner. We hope to be back by sundown.'

Toby and I rode in silence for a time after that. The grass was still lush and green, but it would not be for long. There were still Peebles's cattle on my land, but there would not be for long. Toby said in a quiet voice, 'Tom, maybe you should have told the boys to come along with us. I've a feeling our welcome is not going to be a warm one.'

Maybe Toby was right. Maybe all of them were right and I was behaving foolishly, but I had my plan laid out and I meant to follow it as well as I could. I had spent months thinking this over, remembering the faces of the young hopeful settlers I had guided into this beautiful valley, newlyweds, young children, weary men who had been given some hope of a new life.

I would continue.

At mid-afternoon we crossed the town line and rode up the main street, still puddled here and there by the recent rain. Toby directed me to the printing office where the Stratton *Gazette* was printed. I swung down wearily from the gray horse and tramped on in, leaving Toby with the horses, his eyes watching the passers-by warily.

The gilt sign on the half-paned door proclaimed the name of the newspaper and in smaller script offered: 'Brian Gerwig, Sole Prop.'

I pushed on through the door to find Brian Gerwig, not busily at work as I had expected, but tilted back in a green-leather chair behind a shabby desk, staring dreamily at an old platen printing-press as if it might magically begin turning out the news by itself.

Gerwig was not small, not large. He wore spectacles pushed up on his forehead. He was more boyish-looking than I had imagined. Rather than being startled he shifted his dreamy eyes toward me as if I might have come to rescue him from his frontier life. It's idle to speculate, but he struck me as the sort of young man who had wished to grow up to be a poet, who had come West on a whim and a desire for adventure and found it, on the whole, a dreary and lonely place.

'Yes, sir?' he said, now lowering his eyeglasses to distort his pale-gray eyes.

'I want to place a public notice in tomorrow's paper,' I told him.

'Oh?' he said without interest.

'A half-page should do it.'

'A half-page.' He goggled at me through the lenses of his spectacles. 'Do you know what that will cost you?'

'No, I don't. You tell me.'

'You're serious, aren't you?' he asked, focusing now on my eyes.

'Very.'

'All right.' He shoved a sheet of foolscap toward me across his desk along with inkwell and pen. 'Write out what you want printed.'

I did, carefully. Gerwig watched me intently, at times trying to read what I was writing upside down When I was finished I handed the paper back to him. He studied it with a frown and then a hint of alarm.

'I can't print that!'

'Of course you can,' I said calmly. 'I intend to pay you for it.'

His fingers ran spiderlike over his dark hair. 'But, you don't understand. . . .' he said miserably.

'Yes,' I said, 'I do. Shelley Peebles may not like it. But you did not write this. I did. And Shelley Peebles already does not like me.' I reached into my pocket and pulled out a ten-dollar goldpiece. 'If this is not acceptable,' I told him coldly, 'there are other currencies.'

He saw the slight movement of my hand toward my walnut-handled Colt .44 and decided gold was preferable.

I stood by as he rearranged the newspaper from how he had intended to run it and set my two-column notice up in bold typeface. The platen turned and clacked and still I waited. The paper was warm, the ink still wet when, satisfied, I read what he had printed:

Notice is hereby given that no cattle, horse or other animal of any kind is allowed to graze north of the seven-mile Stratton Valley marker if not carrying an authorized brand. Further if any unauthorized horse, cattle or other animal is not removed from this land forthwith, it will be considered maverick and subject to seizure or slaughter. Further no unauthorized use of any water or water-

course deriving its source from the Pocono River headwater may be used for any purpose whatsoever without explicit permission of its sole owner.

Tom Quinn

There were beads of perspiration on Brian Gerwig's forehead as he printed out his usual run of one hundred papers. He glanced up at me once and said, 'Peebles will have you killed, you know?'

'I know he'll try,' I answered quietly.

'Mister,' the newspaperman said, 'I have to tell you – you're plain crazy.'

I had heard that so often lately that it was becoming repetitious. Hell, maybe they were all right and it was me who was wrong. It does give a man pause to consider.

After folding two of the one-sheet newspapers into eighths and jamming them into my pocket, I stepped out into the still-bright late afternoon day and nearly walked into Mary Ford's arms.

FIVE

I can't tell whether I was more pleased, upset or puzzled by the unexpected return of the woman I had once wanted to marry. My uncertainty was mirrored in her deep-blue eyes, which searched my face at length.

'I have to talk to you, Tom,' she said, taking my wrist with her small hand. She was wearing a yellow dress with lace at the cuffs and throat, and was carrying a yellow parasol. The color suited her. Small tendrils of blond hair slipped from under her white bonnet and were teased by the breeze.

'All right,' I said as calmly as I could.

'Not here,' Mary said with a glance at Toby Trammel, who was still holding the horses, looking down and away as if we were both invisible to him. 'Let's walk uptown a little way.'

Then Toby did look up with a slight warning

glance. I felt Mary's hand slip under my arm at the elbow and she quite definitely, if lightly, turned me away from Toby. We walked uptown along the boardwalk, once again passing the dying sycamore tree I had planted in the town square. The new brick city building appeared and I halted.

'What is it, Tom?'

'This is far enough. Are there still benches in the square?'

'Of course!' She looked ready to laugh – at what I couldn't say. Continuing to cling to my arm, twirling her yellow parasol, she guided me across the square to where a few unpainted wooden benches sat in the broken shade of the old tree. As we reached a bench I removed my bandanna and spread it out for her to sit on. I now had to squint into the sunlight to see her face; I could read no expression in her eyes. The sycamore, like a lost memory, sighed in the breeze.

'Is it going to storm in the high country, Tom?' Mary Ford asked me.

'It might. It's an unpredictable time of year.'

'I thought I heard thunder in the high pass earlier.' I couldn't tell whether she was probing me or simply making the usual mundane conversation a person does when trying to delay getting to the point.

'There's something you wanted to say to me, Mary,' I prompted. I had my eyes on a group of shabby-looking men wearing their guns low, watching us from across the grassless park.

'A lot of things, Tom,' she said, her small hands folding together on her lap. She turned her eyes down briefly. 'You're still a fine-looking man, you know? Your eyes, your face looking as if the elements had chiseled and honed them.'

I didn't respond. I never know what to say to words like those. I only had one question, and I needed to know the answer before the conversation went any further. I met her eyes directly.

'Why did you leave me, Mary?'

She shrugged and managed to make it a charming gesture. 'It's just the way you are, Tom. Reckless and wild. A woman needs some security in her life – especially out in this country! If you had taken the job the railroad offered you in Denver, perhaps we could have gotten back together. Tom, I have seen you when you're pushed, when you feel threatened you're a crazy man.'

'My recklessness is what brought the original settlers to this town, what got us through a few shooting scrapes. Or don't you remember those months on the trail?'

'Of course I do!' she said. 'That was what made me love you. You were so bold and sure of yourself when no other man in the company knew the wild country.'

'But now. . . ?'

Her hand rested lightly on mine and I felt the return of old stirrings that I tried to suppress.

'Don't you see, Tom? Times have changed. The days of the rough trailsmen are passing. We have built a town here; things are settled. The long-trail is gone. I suffered enough deprivation on the way West. I want order and peace in my life. You still want to charge about with guns and war cries. Things aren't like that now. In Stratton we now have a judge, a sheriff, law and order. It's a new era, Tom. Men like Shelley Peebles know that, that the West is changing. Have you met Shelley?'

'I've seen him,' I said carefully, noting that Mary had called him 'Shelley' and not 'Mr Peebles.'

I didn't like the way this conversation was tending. I guess that vague hope of a reconciliation lingered even then, but what if I told her that I was starting a range war, had men ready to shoot it out with the robber barons, had blown up the town's water supply? That would endear me to her, all right! Hell, maybe Mary was right in her thinking. We certainly did not seem destined ever to reach an understanding of matters. She liked the town life too much, it seemed; I could never persuade her to move upcountry to the stone house, far away from the shops and conveniences. I saw that now. A sort of heavy sadness began to settle over me.

'What is it you wanted to say to me, Mary?' I asked wearily.

'My brothers. Ben and Will are with you, aren't they?' she said.

'Yes.'

'You'll kill them one way or the other, won't you?' she demanded with unexpected heat.

'No one needs to be killed at all,' I answered slowly, wondering what Mary did know, how concerned she really was about Big Will and Ben, whether Shelley Peebles hadn't put her up to probing me about my plans. These thoughts were ultimately depressing. There is little so sad as realizing that someone you knew – loved – is not at all what you thought they were. *I have to be wrong*, I thought as her guileless blue eyes met mine again, but then she gave herself away.

'Why then are you and your men driving Shelley's steers off their grazing land?'

'So he did send you,' I said with deep regret.

'I don't know what you mean,' she said flippantly, her hand falling away from mine.

'Yes, you do,' I said, searching her eyes again. 'You can tell Peebles for me that the reason those beeves are being driven south is because they are on my land. Or,' I added, rising to my feet, 'have him read tomorrow's newspaper.'

The stiffness in Mary's voice was cutting. 'Is there anything else I should tell him, Mr Quinn?'

'Yes,' I replied, 'tell him for me that the town of Stratton better get started digging itself some deep water wells.'

Then I spun away on my heel, leaving the puzzled girl in the yellow dress to watch after me. All right, I knew it then. I had been played for a fool. Not the first man in history to have it done to him, but like every other man I had believed – sincerely – that Mary Ford was above such ploys, that she was different. I was three strides away from the boardwalk when I saw Toby Trammel riding down the street, hard, leading my gray. He yelled out to me:

'Watch it, Tom! They've laid an ambush!'

I saw that the loungers I had been watching earlier had disappeared from view. I guessed that they had taken cover in the nearby alley, and as I rolled into the saddle of my gray horse, I pointed warningly at it to Toby and we turned rapidly away. Ten – a dozen – shots rang out from the mouth of the alleyway. We didn't try to fire back, not from the backs of our hard-running horses. We simply spurred toward the outskirts of town at a flat-out gallop.

Half a mile on we drew our sweating ponies up in the shade of a cottonwood grove. I unsheathed my carbine and watched our backtrail as Toby cursed.

'Dirty bushwhackers. Rotten bastards,' he was muttering. 'They creased my pony's neck.'

I glanced at the wounded hammerhead sorrel, judged the wound to be superficial and told him, 'I brought some carbolic with our supplies, Toby. He'll be OK.'

'Rotten bastards,' Toby said again. His hand was shaking as he stroked his beloved horse,

'You know, Toby,' I told him as the wind whispered in the cottonwood trees, 'things are not going to get any easier. They're going to get a hell of a lot worse, in fact. If you want to ride away from it, it's still all right with me.'

The blond wrangler looked up at me with unshakeable intent, 'Tom – you couldn't drive me away now.'

The sun was heeling over toward the peaks of the high mountains before we reached the house. The snowcaps were flushed to crimson and the light scattered by the dying sun seemed cold, casting cruel shadows beneath the pines. The river had unmistakably withered, I noticed with grim satisfaction. The watercourses were barely trickling.

Toby and I had spoken little on the way back to the ranch. He could read my mood, and I saw that his was not much better. I didn't like the look of the house at our homecoming.

The plank door was bolted; the boys had forted up. There were three horses I did not recognize hitched to our rail and two men I did not know sitting on the porch. That meant there was one man concealing himself somewhere.

'Be alert,' I told Toby Trammel, and I saw him unbutton his heavy coat to make his Colt accessible.

'Do you know them?' I asked Toby. He squinted into the low sun and after a moment nodded.

'Lawmen, Tom.'

My mouth tightened. I hadn't meant for this sort of trouble to begin so soon. As we reached the yard, I saw that Toby was right. Sunlight glinted off a star pinned to the coat of a walrus-mustached man who was watching our approach, hands on hips.

'That's Sheriff Langdon,' Toby said in a lowered voice. 'You wouldn't know him. He rode in with Peebles.'

I nodded, slowed my gray horse and looked around, wondering whether the boys inside the house were watching from the slit windows, wondering where the third lawman was concealed. I drew up within ten feet of my porch but did not swing down immediately.

'Good evening, gentlemen,' I said. 'Need something?'

'Need someone to answer the door,' Langdon said. His voice was muffled by a chaw of tobacco. His mustache, I saw now, was streaked with gray. He was a bulky, broad-shouldered man with an air of arrogance.

'Sorry. It was by my orders that they locked themselves down.'

The sheriff took another heavy step forward, spat tobacco juice on the porch planks and asked me, 'You're Tom Quinn, then?'

'I am.'

'You're the man I came to see, Quinn. I thought you were hiding from me.'

'Why would I do that, Sheriff? I've committed no crimes.'

'Can we talk then?' the lawman asked. Still I sat my horse and Toby Trammel remained where he had been, his fingers inches from the butt of his revolver.

'I don't mind,' I told the big-shouldered man,

73

'but it would be more comfortable, and more friendly of you if you'd call your other deputy out of hiding. I'm not fond of concealed guns.'

The sheriff's mustache twitched only slightly in what might have been the briefest of smiles. 'All right,' he agreed. 'Jake! Come on out!'

I shifted my eyes briefly to watch as a scarecrow of man with a Winchester in his hands emerged from the stable. Then, nodding to Toby, I swung down, led my horse to the hitch rail and tied him there.

'Let's go inside, Sheriff. Your two men can make themselves comfortable out here as best they can.' I paused before adding, 'They should know that there are armed men watching from every one of the windows.'

'I figured as much,' Langdon said laconically.

'I remind you just so that they don't take a notion to get up to any mischief.'

Langdon briefly conferred with his deputies and then I called to the house: 'It's Tom, boys. Open up!'

I heard the bar being thrown and the heavy door creaked open. Inside the stone house were Barney Weber, Randall Holt and Big Will Ford. I did not know where Ben Ford and George Holt were, but I suspected they were out in the forest with their rifles at the ready, watching the activity.

I smiled inwardly. The sniper in the stable probably would not have had a chance if he had chosen to try ambushing Toby and me.

I languidly poured coffee for Sheriff Langdon and myself, and settled into my favorite chair. 'What's this about?' I asked him.

'Rustling, for one thing,' he said with gravity.

I couldn't help myself – I laughed out loud.

'Sheriff,' I apologized, 'I'm sorry, but this is the first time I've ever heard of a man being charged with rustling for driving cattle *off* his land!'

Langdon was nonplussed. Maybe his superiors had sent him out to intimidate me without giving him a true picture of the way matters lay. He found his voice again.

'Then there's simple trespassing, Quinn,' he told me in his low voice.

I shook my head and rose, walking to the thin lock-box I always carried with me. Opening it, I returned to my chair, stretching out my hand to give Langdon a pair of folded papers. 'I know you haven't been in this country long, Sheriff. But your bosses must know that I have held this land for seven years, having inherited it from Gil Stratton. This is my land to do with as I like. The only trespassing done around here is being done by Peebles's riders – who, by the way, had better keep their distance unless they are employed in the honest work of driving cattle off my graze.'

Langdon slowly read the legal documents I had handed him. I couldn't tell if he was near-sighted or simply unused to reading. He squinted, wiped his eye with a finger, sighed and tugged at his walrus mustache. The expression on his face was that of a man who felt he has been duped. Maybe he had, maybe he was just temporarily buffaloed.

'I'll have to take these papers into Stratton for Judge Manx to review,' he said slowly.

'No, you don't,' I said firmly, reaching for the documents. 'A notarized copy of my deed is on file at the courthouse. There's another copy in the Denver bureau of records. I will keep this one, if you don't mind.'

I don't know if he had meant to destroy the deed, believing that thereby my claim might be invalidated, but he nodded heavily and handed it back to me. The reason I had filed not only at the courthouse but also had had a certified copy sent to the capital was because old Gil Stratton had advised me to on his death-bed, saying, 'Son, they'll steal your land if they can. *Our* land.' On my own, I never would have thought of it. I was young and inexperienced. Gil must have had a similar bad experience somewhere in his long life. Now there was no way anyone could dispute my claim to the land or take it from me.

Unless they killed me.

Sheriff Langdon sat watching me in silence, sipping at his coffee while my men watched out the windows for any sign of threatening activity. 'You plan ahead, don't you, Quinn?' Langdon said at length.

'I try to.'

'One other matter . . .' he hesitated. 'My deputies and I noticed that the water flow up here is slowing to nothing. Like the Pocono's suddenly gone dry. You have anything to do with that?'

'Nature's unpredictable,' I said.

'So are men,' the sheriff said, rising. 'You know, young man, if they can't take care of you legally, they'll come after you the other way.'

'Will you be with them, Langdon?' I asked.

He didn't answer. Shaking his head heavily he walked to the door, opened it and stepped out without so much as a backward glance.

'It's been a hell of a day,' Toby Trammel murmured.

By the time George Holt and Ben Ford had made their cautious way back to the stone house, young Randall Holt had a pot of stew boiling furiously away on the stove. We gathered again at the table while waiting to eat. I ran briefly through the events of the day for those who had missed a part of them and then assigned new duties.

'We're going to have to start running a night-watch, men. The sheriff is onto us now, so is Peebles. They might not know my intent, but they know enough to understand that we mean trouble for them. We need two men up at a time every night. You can divide the schedule up any way you like, just so we have watchers. I don't know what they might try.'

I left the boys discussing how they were going to work out the shifts and tramped along the hall to the small bedroom that had been Gil's and was now mine. Further along the corridor was the bunk area, set up for six men, then a pantry that was seldom used for there was also one in the kitchen. Still, if a person was going to winter-up through long, snow-bound months, the extra storage space would prove useful.

I didn't know whether I would be there over the winter. I didn't know whether I would be there next week. Alive. I lay on the bed and stared at the faint glimmer of starlight I could see through the high, slit window and the haze of the sky beyond and wondered, more deeply than anyone else, if I wasn't making a string of bad choices. More than that, whether I had done right by persuading these trusting men to follow along.

I might have accomplished nothing other than to drag these loyal men to the brink of destruction.

SIX

I rode out early that morning with Toby Trammel at my side. I wanted to see for myself how the job of driving the cattle past the seven-mile marker was coming along, and to study the trail north for any horse tracks that did not belong there. Ben Ford and young Randall Holt had ridden out earlier to continue the job of hieing the beeves toward the south. Big Will Ford and George Holt who had taken the last shift on night-watch were still asleep in the bunk room. Barney Weber was keeping himself busy with yard chores and generally keeping an eye out for incoming riders.

The day was cold and bleak. Even though I had brought it about myself, it was surprising how lonesome the empty land looked. No bright new sunlight on the fading river, the snaking rills throttled, no cattle grazing peacefully in the long grass.

I wandered through my meditations deep in thought. It was a surprise when Toby lifted a pointing finger and reined in sharply, saying, 'Something's up, Tom!'

I shifted my eyes to see Ben Ford flagging his black horse on either flank with his reins, riding hell-bent toward us. He was hatless and wild-eyed. He drew his lathered horse up beside us.

'They got him, Tom!' Ben eventually managed to pant.

'Who? What happened, Ben. Take a minute, will you?'

The black horse shuddered with exhaustion. There was perspiration glistening on Ben's forehead.

Calming slightly, he told us: 'Young Randall Holt. They killed him, Tom. We had split up to drive two small bunches of cattle south. After I reached the seven-mile marker I turned back to find Randall, thinking he might need some help. I found him – dead.'

'Shot down?' I asked coldly.

'No. Come on, I'll show you.'

At a slower gait, Ben led us across the muddy remains of a creekbed and into a grove of white oak trees beyond. There we found Randall Holt, his hands strapped behind his back, his body hanging from a noose around his neck. I cursed and swung down urgently, although I knew the need for haste was long past. Young Randall Holt was dead. Lynched. Killed before he had ever even matured enough to put a razor to his face.

'Did you see anyone, Ben?' I asked the trembling man who stood beside me.

He shook his head heavily. 'No one, Tom. I shouldn't have left him working alone.'

'You didn't do anything wrong,' Toby told the anguished man. Toby still sat his sorrel, hands crossed on the pommel. I caught his eye and his meaning. If whoever did this had caught them together, we likely would have two men swinging from the oak-limb instead of one.

'Cut him down,' I instructed Toby, who edged his wary horse nearer, unsheathed his Bowie knife and sawed through the new hemp of the rope. I tried to soften the fall of the body, but still it dropped with a sickening thud onto the dark earth.

'Now what?' Toby asked.

'Ride back and tell George what's happened to his brother.'

'And what are you going to do, Tom?'

'Take Randall home,' I told him, looking up through the tangled growth of the old oak tree at the cold sky. 'Look around and see if you can find his little paint pony, would you?'

The horse was nowhere to be found and so, with Toby's and Ben's help, the body of Randall Holt was hoisted up over the withers of my gray. That patient animal shied a little. I don't know if it was the extra weight he objected to or the near scent of death.

The sun continued its descent toward the snowy mountain peaks. The long shadows of my horse and its sad burden stretched out before me as I entered the Gunnison Notch cut-off. The pine-trees crowded close around me, black as sin except in their highest reaches where the last sunlight touched the treetops with pure gold. The forest was cold and silent. I rode with a heaviness I cannot describe.

What was I going to tell Sadie Holt? Her husband had been killed – some might have blamed me for that. Now her younger son was gone. And some might blame me for that. I steeled myself against the woman's grief, anger, collapse, whatever was to come as I emerged from the eastern end of the cut-off and rode into the yard of the Holt ranch at purple dusk.

I swung down from the gray horse, wanting to say a few words to Sadie before she was forced to deal with actual sight of the body. The door to the little house stood open. Frowning, I rested my hand on the butt of my Colt and paused, looking around. I saw no horses, no signs of trouble. There was no fire burning in the hearth and the wind was cold; why then was the door open wide?

I stepped up onto the porch carefully, ready for anything. Anything but what I did find.

Young Julia Holt was seated in a rocking-chair before the cold fireplace, her reddish hair loose around her shoulders, slowly, slowly rocking.

'Julia?' I said softly. She did not turn her head to look at me. 'Where's your mother? I'm afraid . . . I have some bad news for her.'

'Good,' Julia said in a low, wooden voice and I just stared at her, turning my hat in my hands.

'I don't understand you.'

'It's good that she isn't here to receive it,' she said, turning her head slightly toward me.

'She isn't? Where did she go, Julia?'

'No one knows that, do they?' Then she bowed her face to her hands and began to weep. Through the rush of tears, she said, 'She's in her bed, Tom. She won't have to receive any more bad news ever again. At about three this afternoon,' she told me, wiping her nose with a small handkerchief, 'Mother passed away.'

'She. . . .' I found it hard to speak. Sadie had always seemed strong, indomitable despite the hardships she had endured. Another thought kept me in dumb amazement.

It had been about three o'clock when Randall Holt had been lynched.

'I'd better go ahead and tell you then,' I said, drawing up a chair so that I faced Julia, and I went on, telling her about her brother. At one minute she was stony-faced, at the next she collapsed into sobbing. And, from time to time, I also saw in those green eyes, a flicker of anger – at me? the killers? the world? I could not say.

After a while Julia's outer grief subsided. I could not think of a thing to say to assuage her inner pain. 'I'll see to the burying in the morning,' I told her. 'What will you do, Julia?'

'What is there to do?' she asked with a small hysterical laugh.

'You can't stay here. Not any longer.'

'No. But there is nowhere else.' Her dejection was profound.

'I'll build a fire,' I said, rising. 'It's going to be a chill night.' Working with my hands kept my thoughts away from the tragedy of the family. Before bringing in firewood, I unsaddled and stabled my gray horse. Randall's body I placed in the tool shed, latching it firmly to prevent any wild animal's incursion. Then I gathered an armload of wood from the pile – which, I noticed was greatly depleted, returned to the house and built a fire.

Julia had risen from the chair and was making coffee, her eyes haunted, her movements mechanical. I seated myself, watching her and the flickering fire alternately. When she returned with two tin cups of coffee, I broached the matter I had been considering.

'You know you can't stay here alone. You're welcome to come up to my ranch, Julia.'

She stared at the flames in the fireplace, crimson and gold, curling and twining among the logs. 'That hardly seems proper,' she commented at last.

'Your brother, George, is up there. Toby Trammel and Barney Weber. You know them. You'll be all right, much safer than you would be here alone. I can provide you with your own room . . . just until you can decide what it is you want to do next.'

She sipped carefully at her coffee, her eyes shifting only once to me before returning to the mesmeric flames. 'I'll think it over, Tom,' she said at last. 'There really isn't any place else, is there?'

I spent the night in the room that George and Randall had shared as boys, anger at what had happened waking me at intervals. I rose in the cold of pre-dawn, nudged the fire to life and went to the shed to begin my unhappy chore.

We started out at mid-morning, Julia riding her

little pinto pony, leaving behind us an empty house and two more sad mounds of earth beside the grave of Tyler Holt.

Just past noon we drew up in front of the stone house. Barney Weber, with his rifle in his hand, opened the door and stood there frowning as I took Julia's little carpetbag containing her few belongings and helped her down from her horse.

'Is George here?' I asked.

'Still asleep. He had the late shift.'

Barney's frown remained in place as he nodded and turned back into the house. I followed with Julia who looked around the house, now swept and scrubbed, actually looking better than when Gil and I had lived there alone. There was an Indian blanket hanging above the big stone fireplace, a few more scattered across the plank floor. The boys had cleaned their dishes off the table and washed them. Julia said nothing, just stood there, clutching her bag, but she seemed relieved. Maybe she had expected much worse.

After a minute Barney returned, and behind him a tousled, sleep-drugged George Holt. He stiffened and came alert suddenly at the sight of his sister standing beside me.

'Tom! What the hell are you thinking, bringing Julia up here?'

'There was no choice,' I said calmly, hearing the anger in George's voice. 'Why don't you two go into my room where you can be alone. She'll tell you about it.'

Barney continued to eye me dubiously. I could read his thoughts. They were the same as George's. What was I doing bringing a young woman up here when we all knew there was bound to be trouble? I didn't bother to explain things to him just then.

'Who's out?' I asked.

'The Ford brothers are riding the perimeter. Toby was up late, too; he's still in bed.'

'All right. I'm going to find something to eat. Saddle up your pony. You and I will spell Big Will and Ben so that they can have some dinner.'

Barney's eyes were still fixed questioningly on me. He nodded and started toward the door, and at that moment we heard a high mournful wail that faded to a groan coming from my room. George knew now. Barney's frown deepened further. I still told him nothing. The word would get around.

I did say, 'After you've seen to the horses, Barney, take my gear and toss it into the bunk room. I'll be sleeping in Randall's old bed. Julia's taking my room.' That seemed to ease his mind a little. I have no idea what he had been thinking, what George thought at first, but I was beyond caring. I went into the kitchen, scraped some cold biscuits out of the pan and poured myself a cup of coffee, watching the slash of cold sunlight that cut through the narrow slit window in the stone wall fall across the table and floor, dust motes dancing in its blue shaft.

What now, I asked myself, brooding. I had boasted to and infuriated Pebbles. I had stirred up a hornet's nest, but that was all I had accomplished. What were we to do now? Wait until a gang of armed men showed up to kill more of us, to keep us forted up until our supplies ran out – Toby and I hadn't mule-packed up enough to last five men . . . and a woman, long. Men with rifles in the woods could even keep us from reaching the well in back of the house.

Without conscious decision, I knew already what I had to do. I could not let them dictate the rules of battle. I had to take it to them.

George appeared, looking haggard and beaten. His eyes were red, his movements were unsteady. I let him pour himself a cup of coffee and sit down. He was going to be of little use today, I knew.

'Stay with your sister this morning, all right, George? Watch the place. Barney is going with me. Ben and Will should be riding in in about an hour.' He only nodded, his elbows on the table, hands on his head. I felt like saying something of comfort, but I knew no appropriate words.

'Do you mind if I take your black, George? My horse could use some rest.'

He waved a hand unconcernedly, his thoughts deep and far away. The woman who had nursed him, dressed him, comforted him was gone. His brother was dead. The world was a bleak and lonely place. I rose from my chair, briefly put my hand on his slumped shoulder and reminded him:

'You've got to take care of Julia now. You're all she has.'

I got little response. Barney had come back in a few minutes earlier. As I put on my hat and started out, I saw him taking my bedroll and a sackful of goods from my bedroom to the bunk room. I waited for his return.

'Ready?' I asked the freckle-faced kid.

'I suppose . . .' he hesitated, looking back down the hallway toward my room. 'I just gathered up as much stuff I could see that was yours. I might have left something behind. Tom,' he said lifting his doleful eyes to mine, 'it's awful to hear a woman cry like that, isn't it?'

Barney and I rode southward to relieve the Ford brothers. Bamey's trepidation had returned.

I couldn't blame him a lot, but I couldn't afford to just have him sitting around the house every day. I needed men willing to fight, and if he wasn't, well, instead of asking him if he wanted to leave next time, I'd have to tell him that it would be best if he did.

The storm clouds were still dark and thick above the high peaks, but I did not think it would rain. The wind was as cold as ever. George Holt's little black horse – the one with the white stocking on its left foreleg, moved nimbly and eagerly underneath me. It was a little too slender in the legs for my liking, but I could see why a man would favor it.

We met the Fords near the oak-grove where we had found Randall Holt hanging from a tree. Both of them looked weary, and that was one more problem that had to be solved. I couldn't expect the men to stand night-watch and still be fresh for a day's work the next morning.

Both of the Fords were standing beside their horses, big Will with his hat tilted back, watching our approach. Ben appeared agitated about something, but he did not speak.

'Nothin',' Will replied to my enquiry. 'Only a few stragglers from the herd ranging about. Sooner or later they'll realize that the rest of the cattle have drifted south and they'll follow them.'

'Any of the Peebles riders about?' I asked.

'No, Tom,' Will told me, shrugging his heavy shoulders, 'we haven't seen a single man. Some horse-tracks along the dry creek, but they're old, look like they've been there for days.'

Ben at last gave voice to what had been troubling him. 'Tom, why are we bothering any more? Peebles's cattle have been hied south. Everyone is beat. We can fort up forever in your house, but it doesn't look like anyone's even coming, like they care. We're short on supplies; we all know that. In a few days we'll just be criss-crossing your land doing nothing at all, growing hungry.'

From the expression on Will's face I could tell that the brothers had been discussing this between them. Now Will did speak up.

'It seems to us, Tom, that the conversation you had with Sheriff Langdon did the trick.' His deep voice was almost apologetic. 'They know now that you have every right to be here; that they don't. I don't think Peebles cares one way or the other. He knows you aren't going to run cattle up here, that there's nothing they need to do to run you off. After a while, after winter has settled in, you won't even be able to support yourself, let alone hold onto the land.'

'They'll offer you a fair price for your land, Tom,' Ben put in, 'and you'll have to take it. If you ask me, you've already won.'

I studied the faces of Mary's brothers. I had counted on them without realizing that they were not committed to my fight out of any sense of loyalty, but simply because it had been a paying job. Will looked down at his boots.

'You boys going in to dinner?' I asked, knowing what the answer would be.

'No, Tom,' Big Will said without looking up. 'I guess we'll be riding.'

'What do you figure I owe you?' I dug into the purse I carried inside my buffalo coat.

'I don't know, Tom. . . .' Will answered.

'Two dollars a day?'

'That'll do it,' big Will agreed. I thumbed a few silver dollars into my palm and placed them into Will's thick, calloused hand. 'Tom, we don't want you to think—'

'You did your work; you made your choice,' I said coldly. Will nodded and both of the Ford brothers swung into leather, riding out through the cold dappled shade of the oaks. They had every right to go, but my chances of protecting my land if Peebles did decide to try to drive me off had just taken a huge setback.

I was aware of Barney Weber shifting uncomfortably in his saddle, watching the Fords ride away. I looked into the freckle-faced boy's eyes and I didn't have to ask. Barney had been jittery since the first day. I said nothing. I opened my purse again and slid silver into his hand.

'Tom, I'm sorry,' he said nervously, 'but you did tell me that if I was ever feeling that I was ready to ride away. . . .'

'Yes, I did,' I answered as gently as possible. 'I told you there would be no shame attached, no hard feelings.'

'Still, Tom. . . .'

'Get on your way, saddle tramp,' I said lightly. I smiled and slapped his pony's rump, and with only a single glance back, he rode away, following in the tracks of Ben and Will Ford.

I watched for a long minute and thought, *I'm a hell of a general.*

I rode the southern line for a few hours, seeing nobody, no unusual tracks, then turned for home as the sun began to lower its bright face behind the dark mountains. In a bleak mood I put George's horse up in the stable, paused to stroke the muzzle of my gray and walked to the house. The fire in the hearth was new and bright, burning almost smokelessly. Toby was up now, stretching and yawning at the table, coffee-cup before him. George, looking somewhat collected, but worried, watched me as I entered and barred the door. At the stove Julia, blue apron wrapped around her, her red hair pinned up, was watching a simmering stew bubble in the black iron pot. She glanced at me without making eye contact.

'The boys never came in for dinner,' George said worriedly as I seated myself on one of the kitchen chairs.

'No,' I had to tell them. 'They pulled out. Barney, too.'

'Barney!' Toby said with astonishment that settled into disappointment. 'All you did was try to help him out of the stables, Tom.'

I shrugged. 'He didn't like the way things were shaping up.'

'And Ben and big Will?' George Holt asked tightly.

'Same with them, I guess.' I said, moving my elbow slightly as Julia placed a cup of fresh coffee on the table beside my arm. 'They couldn't see the logic in risking their necks for a fight that isn't their own. I think that what happened to Randall brought it home to them.' I looked at each of them in turn and said, 'Nobody has to stay here – it's my war.'

With unexpected ferocity, Julia whirled toward me. Her hands were quivering, her green eyes sparking with intensity. 'Your war!' she exploded 'What about me! What about George? We've lost a father, a mother, a brother. This is our war, too. We're going nowhere. If you'd give me a shotgun, I'd ride with you, the same as my mother wanted to do the day after the night-riders overran us and killed Dad.'

Her temper cooled slowly as she turned her back to us and returned to unnecessary kitchen chores. I was startled by the heat in her words, and found myself admiring the red-headed girl more and more. I smiled lopsidedly at George who still appeared shaken by recent events. He answered without looking at me.

'Don't even ask me, Tom,' he said. 'My sister said what I would have told you—' he half-smiled, glancing her way '—if not in that way. I'm sticking, count on it.'

Toby Trammel was tilted back in one of the wooden chairs. Lazily the blond wrangler said, 'I already told you, Tom. You'd have to drive me away before I'd quit on you.'

'All right, then,' I said, standing before the low-burning fire for a while, staring at the curlicued flames. 'Better draw some extra water from the well. There's no telling what Peebles's next move might be.'

I walked to the gunrack and took down my left-hand holster and spare Colt, belting it on cross-wise to the other. The three of them watched me silently. It was Julia who spoke.

'Tom, what are you doing?'

'Just sprucing up a little. I can't be attending an important function half-dressed.'

SEVEN

'You're going into Stratton?' Toby Trammel asked. He was already on his feet, reaching for his coat and hat.

'Alone, Toby,' I told him. 'Three of you is barely enough to hold the fort here.'

Toby looked doubtful. What I had said was true, but everyone knew that I alone was hardly a match for Peebles's dozen hand-picked killers.

George was obviously disturbed as well. 'Tom,' he said, 'it's a rough trail, and we have a late-rising moon these nights.'

'I know. But I've ridden that trail more than any man in this country. My horse knows the way as well. Besides, having the moon behind me would only make my silhouette that much clearer. If there's anyone down the trail looking for me, there's a chance I can pass unseen.'

'A chance. . . !' George Holt said unhappily.

Julia's quiet voice interrupted him.

'He's going, George. His mind is made up, can't you see? Once his mind is made up, there's no point in trying to talk Tom Quinn out of anything.'

She was right, of course, but it gave me pause to wonder why. Was I simply too bull-headed to listen to good advice offered with good intentions? I didn't know. I saddled my gray horse in the gloom of night, carefully strapping my heavy saddle-bags on behind, with their explosive contents, and started south upon the long trail, my rifle riding loosely across the horse's withers.

The absence of moonlight caused the blanket of stars to shine brightly like clustered diamonds, visible even through the dark branches of the Douglas fir and blue spruce along the trail. The heavy scent of the pines was nearly smothering. There were no sounds but the gentle clopping of the gray's hoofs, the creak of the trees swaying in the night wind, and once the astonishingly loud complaint of a low-swooping great horned owl.

I had gone a mile from the house when the crack of a large-bore rifle shattered the silence of the mountain night. Almost simultaneously I saw the flash of red-yellow from the muzzle of a gun on the wooded slope above me.

The bullet was near enough to tug the skirt of

my buffalo-hide coat. I kicked out of the stirrups as the gray danced under me and I landed in a clumsy roll on the pine-needle-littered earth. I expected a second shot, a third, but none followed the first. Perhaps I had dropped out of their line of sight and now, in the moonless night, was merely another dark hummock against the forest floor. The gray had trotted on for a short distance. Now I saw it pause and look back at me wondering what sort of man-game this was that we were playing. As did I.

I had my rifle in my hand. Now, as silently as possible, I levered a round into the receiver. I heard no movement in all of the dark forest rising around me. I understood their dilemma. Had that single shot killed me, or was I waiting there in the darkness to ambush my ambushers? Their next move would depend on how anxious they were to kill me.

I lay on my belly, unmoving for long minutes. I was shivering now although the night was no colder than it had been. Through the ranks of pines I could still see the stars, beaming brightly. I did not move. My muscles began to cramp, my eyes to weary from my constant, searching stare. My brow perspired despite the chill of the evening.

Nothing moved, no sound murmured in the

night except for the wind ruffling the pines. A pine-cone fell near at hand and the sound was unnaturally loud. I could detect no movement, hear no footsteps, no whispered words.

I waited.

If they really wanted me they would have to come down the flank of the wooded hill to where the trail wound its way through the tall forest. I looked to my gray horse to assure myself that it had not wandered off, and at that moment I saw its ears twitch, one turning in the direction of the slope above me. I eased myself into a better shooting position; raising myself on my left elbow, I curled my hand loosely around the checked fore-end of my Winchester's stock, remaining prone.

Still nothing. No sound of shuffling boots, of whispered instructions. If they were moving toward me, they were as silent as Indians. I wristed the sweat from my eyes and waited. I would not be the first to move. They knew where I was, where they thought I was. I had no idea where they had gotten to.

Then I did. Watching from the forest verge to the ridge of the slope, I saw a single brilliant star shining through the Douglas firs. I saw it. And then I didn't. Something, someone had passed in front of the star, momentarily blocking its silver light. I shifted my rifle sights that way. There was a small but unmistakable sound to my left, lower on the hillslope. A boot had broken a fallen pine-twig. I smiled despite my perilous position. I had thought all along that there were two men out there. Now I had a reasonable idea where each of them was. Also I had learned that they were not just trying to frighten me.

They were determined to finish the job.

Why else would a man slip around in the dark-ness knowing that there was a good possibility that his prey was alive, was certainly armed and deadly. No, these two wanted me dead, there was no doubt about it. I wondered idly if Peebles had put a bounty on my head and considered it quite possible. I again ran the cuff of my coat over my forehead and waited. There are few tasks more unnerving and demanding than waiting for death. The patience of a man has its limits, and I had to fight the urge to leap up and run, to try to make it to my horse, to flee into the darkness of the forest, no matter that logic told me that remaining where I was was the best plan if I were to survive.

He loomed up, not that far away from me. The man on my left, he who had broken the twig underfoot, emitted a muffled, surprised grunt as he emerged from the forest edge and recognized my dark form for what it was. He lifted his rifle to his shoulder and fired. My rifle had spoken a split second earlier, and I was the more ready. As his long gun spewed fire and his bullet dug a deep furrow in the dark earth, I shot him in the chest. I heard him gasp above the racketing echoes of our shots, stagger back and fall flat on his back. He said a few words through the blood in his mouth, but I could not make them out, nor did they matter any more to anyone in this world.

I eased to the side inch by inch, just enough to change position in case the bushwhacker on the hillslope had located me by my muzzle flash. I waited for the second man to make his move as the minutes in the forest crept past with infinite slowness.

I had no warning. The ambusher was a hell of a woodsman. He burst from the forest, rifle at his waist, levering shots through the barrel as fast as it could be fired. Lead sang past me, spattered cold earth into my face and eyes. He was a woodsman, but no marksman. Had the sight of his friend going down driven him to reckless fury? There was no telling, but he had emptied half of his magazine during his wild charge without penetrating flesh and bone.

I centered my bead-sight on his chest and fired. I missed the heart, shooting up as I was from my prone position, but he screamed out, dropped his rifle and clutched at his throat. It was a neck shot I saw immediately, as I rose to my feet and rushed him. My legs moved awkwardly, stiff and slow from lying still for so long against the cold earth. I did not want this man to die; there were questions he could answer for me.

He was still howling with pain and anger when I reached him, but his wound did not appear to be fatal. I had it in mind to tie him up, bandage his neck and then interrogate him. That's what I believed was going to happen next. It's always a good idea to plan; seldom a good idea to project what is bound to happen.

As I stumbled to him on rubbery legs, unconsciously lowering my Winchester, his hand flicked down and came up with a massive Bowie knife, its polished blade gleaming in the starlight. He waved it in front of me and then tried a slashing move which barely missed my throat. Bleeding from the mouth, his feet unsteady under him, he was nevertheless determined to fight to the grave.

He staggered out of position; his loss of blood was telling. I managed to get my left hand on his wrist. I dropped my rifle, took his hand with my right and bent it back on itself sharply. Nothing can be gripped once the hand is folded like that and the Bowie dropped from his fingers. In puzzlement, in pain, in fury he screamed into my face. It was a wordless howl, frustrated pain and mingled hatred. He slipped in my grip and sagged toward the ground. I tried to hold him up, but it was no use.

My unknown attacker slumped away to the ground. In the near-darkness I tried to use my bandanna to bandage his neck, but I knew that it was already too late. In a matter of minutes he lay inert, silent against the earth, his open eyes reflecting the silver starlight.

I rose shakily and whistled the gray up. That stolid animal walked toward me heavily, wondering if this was the end of our games for that night.

Maybe. I just couldn't be sure. It might have been only the beginning. I was still as determined as ever to ride to Stratton. I continued on my way, leaving behind me two dead men whom I had never met, paid killers, men who had gotten exactly what they had deserved. Nevertheless I rode with a vague sense of remorse. Whoever they had been, whatever, they had family, perhaps children and friends somewhere. The taking of life is a terrible thing. I had to remind myself that it was not I who had begun this, but the greedy robber baron, Shelley Peebles, to whom the loss of the lives of these men would mean nothing at all. I might lose sleep that night, but Peebles certainly would not.

It was time to see if I could cause him to miss a little.

It was a riotous night in Stratton when I trailed into town shortly after eight o'clock. The saloons were going full tilt. I rode lazily past the general uproar, the cursing and banjo-playing, the break-ing of glass, twice a gunshot. I was fatigued beyond what I wished to admit. Physically, mentally drained.

No matter, I had come to do a job, and I would do it.

I had considered on the first leg of my journey that however despicable I considered Shelley Peebles, we might be able to work out some mutu-ally agreeable truce. Being ambushed on the trail had erased any conciliatory thoughts I might have had. This was the town I had built. This was the land I had owned. I wanted nothing for profit; I wanted the vermin to be driven out and to restore Stratton to what it had been – a decent place for the young, the old, the decent people to live.

It seemed, now, a futile wish, riding as I was – alone and without resources. Still, something, some impulse deep within me nudged me along the path of retribution.

I knew where I was going even if I did not know why.

Earlier Toby Trammel had pointed out where Shelley Peebles had built his new house, a two-story white-painted wooden structure set about a hundred yards behind the new brick courthouse. I had only glanced at it in passing. Now, approaching it, I studied it deliberately. Porticoed, a front upstairs balcony, set in a grove of cottonwood trees, it was the sort of manorial structure suitable for the robber baron, Stratton's leading citizen and murderer.

Lights blazed from every window. I could hear music. Some sort of celebration or ball was in progress. Frowning, I slowed the gray, noticing the half-dozen surreys and twice that many saddle-horses hitched before the house which was a true mansion in this part of the country.

There was even a balding man in livery, wearing white gloves, waiting on the porch to provide service. I could tell he didn't like my looks by his frowning assessment. He would soon like them even less.

I swung down from my gray horse. The servant started to come forward – to help or complain – I couldn't tell which. I swung out of leather and threw my buffalo coat over the gray's back, behind the saddle. I rolled up both of my red shirt's cuffs and resettled my Colt revolvers in their cross-belted holsters. Tugging my hat down

I approached the porch. The servant had managed to fade away before I had reached it. The white-painted double doors were open and so I walked on in.

There had been music and dancing, but now the men and women in the chandelier-lit great hall paused as one to stare at me. I couldn't blame then. The men wore suits, the ladies were decked out in ball-gowns and jewelry. They couldn't have been expected to welcome an unshaven, rough-looking man weighted down by two pistols.

I knew now where the servant had slipped off to. From a side room Shelley Peebles, wearing a frozen frown entered, accompanied by a sober-looking Sheriff Langdon in a black suit, and a pigeon-chested man with thinning white hair whom I did not recognize, but took to be Judge Manx.

Lounging against the doorframe behind them was the gunfighter, Kit Stacy, his longish yellow hair slicked down, his buckskins replaced by a dark suit, ruffled shirt and black string-tie.

Peebles's expression was not startled but more embarrassed, I thought, as he glanced at his guests.

'This is a private affair, Quinn. No one invited you.'

'We need to talk, Peebles.'

He looked me up and down from my scuffed boots to my dusty hat. 'You'll have to put your guns up,' he said.

'No. I wouldn't talk to you without them,' I replied.

The expression in the narrow man's eyes hardened. He ran a finger over his thin mustache and nodded.

'All right then, damnit!' he said in a fierce whisper. 'But not here. Come into my office.'

I nodded amiably and we went in a group to an inner room, my hat still firmly in place, my spurs jingling. At some unseen signal the band began to play again and people resumed their dancing, though there was an uncomfortable murmur of voices behind me.

Peebles seated himself in a black leather chair behind a broad ebony desk, not glaring at me, but trying to appraise my intentions, it seemed. The judge sat in a similar chair in the corner of the room, mopping his high forehead with a handkerchief. The sheriff stood grimly in the opposite corner, his beefy arms folded. Kit Stacy was, I knew, positioned behind me. Despite Shelley Peebles's declaration that guns were not allowed in his house, I had noticed a tell-tale bulge beneath the skirt of Stacy's jacket. Peebles, I knew, usually wore a high-riding small-caliber pistol and I doubted that Sheriff Langdon was accustomed to going anywhere without a revolver. What I had said to Peebles was true enough – I wasn't about to enter a closed room with these four unarmed.

'What is it that's troubling you exactly?' Peebles asked in a mild voice. He reached for a thin cigar and lit it while waiting for my answer. I noticed a folded copy of the Stratton *Gazette* on a corner of the desk, my bold-type notice obvious.

'That's simple enough,' I told him, letting my eyes flicker from one man to the next in turn. 'Murder always troubles me, Peebles. More troubling is the fact that we have a sheriff and a judge who look the other way so long as it's you who does the murders.'

'I've never. . . !' Peebles said, half-rising from his chair with mock indignation.

'I'm sorry,' I said coldly, 'I should have said "when your hired killers commit murder".'

'This is slanderous,' the judge said. He had a strangely high-pitched voice for such a portly man. 'Do you have any idea what that is under the law, Quinn?'

'My understanding of it is that it is the uttering of false statement,' I answered. 'Since what I'm saying is the truth it can hardly be considered slander.'

'What murders are you referring to?' Sheriff Langdon asked coldly. He was remaining loyal to his employer, but I thought I saw a shadow of doubt in his brown eyes. I kept my own eyes fixed on Peebles, not putting it past him to reach for a gun and shoot me. There were, after all, three substantial citizens to vouch for anything that might happen in this room.

The thing was, he hadn't the guts to try it while I was wearing my guns. He was not a killer, as he had said. He was willing to let others do that work for him. He would not risk his own life.

I answered Langdon without shifting my eyes from Peebles. 'I'm referring to the murders of Tyler Holt and the recent lynching of his son, Randall. I don't know how many settlers you killed, threatened or drove off before I arrived. I imagine the list is a lot longer. I'm not including the death of Sadie Holt who died out of grief for her husband and young son. That can't be called murder, although you are directly responsible for her death too.'

'A lot of wild accusations,' Peebles said, leaning back in his leather chair. His head was wreathed in blue cigar smoke. 'Have you come to discuss matters or simply to fling unfounded aspersions around?' he demanded.

'Maybe both,' I answered honestly. 'A man likes

to let other people know where they stand in his estimation.'

'Which is?'

'Only a little lower than a rattlesnake.'

While Peebles chewed on that and calculated his next move, I took the time to glance around the room. The sheriff had not moved. His arms still folded, he gazed balefully at me. Judge Manx was again wiping his forehead with a pocket-handkerchief. I knew where Kit Stacy was, and I looked his way. The known gunfighter was watching me with faint amusement in his hooded eyes.

The room had a high, arched ceiling. Behind Peebles's uncluttered desk was a double window with dozens of panes framed in white wood, the carpet underfoot was rust-colored, deeply piled. There was a row of books placed neatly in a carved-oak case along one wall, a scattering of papers on a separate, smaller desk, perhaps for the use of a secretary.

In the corner behind this desk, propped up against the wall, was a frilly yellow parasol.

'What do you propose we do about this?' Peebles asked calmly, flicking ash from his cigar into an agate ashtray.

'First you must promise to keep your cattle and your men off of my land in the future.'

'I believe we have already heard your position

112

on that,' Peebles said, nodding at the *Gazette.*

'I wanted to tell you personally,' I said. 'Any incursions on my land will be met with armed resistance.'

Peebles smiled confidently. 'By all three of you?' he asked with amusement.

How could he. . . ? It was instantly clear how he knew there was only me, George Holt and Toby Trammel to hold the land. Will and Ben Ford must had to have told him! They had been acting as spies for Peebles. They had tried to give me a beating on my first day back in Stratton yet I had accepted their regretful apology and hired them to work for me. On reflection, I probably had done that for Mary's sake.

Pondering this, I felt a cold chill run down my spine. On the day that Randall Holt had been lynched, Ben Ford had been riding with him. And Ben had told me when I asked him that the only sign of tracks of horses along the creek had probably been days old. Meaning there had been only one man who could have murdered Randall.

It sickened me; I should have seen through it. Big Will and Ben had been working for Peebles when I arrived. Their only complaint had been that the robber baron had left them with a scant ten acres of land. Why had he left them any at all? Had they then made a deal to expand their ranch by agreeing to murder?

At Mary's instigation?

I glanced once again at the yellow parasol tilted against the wall in the corner of the room, my heart feeling as though it had turned to stone.

'Let's see what we *can* do to resolve this problem,' Peebles was saying, relighting his cold cigar. 'I still believe we can come to agreement without further violence.' He again touched his mustache, offering me a smile that was wolfish. 'The river has dried up. The graze even in the lower valleys is turning sere and brown. The town has no water resources except the Pocono River. I know that this is your doing, Quinn. . . .'

He would know that through the Ford brothers.

'. . . Towns are formed where there is a water supply, a river, a lake. It's been that way since prehistory. Without water there is no civilization.' Kit Stacy, speaking for the first time, interrupted Peebles's rambling lecture with an irrelevant comment.

'The boys are having to drink their whiskey straight,' the gunman said. No hint of appreciative humor appeared in Peebles's eyes.

'I want that river opened up again, Quinn. I won't accept your action. The judge here tells me that you likely do have the legal right to do what

114

you've done, but I won't see my cattle die or Stratton disappear from the map, becoming just another ghost town in the mountains. No!' he shouted, showing raw emotion for the first time. He lifted a fist as if to bang it down on his desk top, but recovered his composure before he did.

His eyes were narrowed now, and I could see the wolf in them again. 'I'll promise to leave your land, your people alone if you open the Pocono again.'

'If I don't?' I asked and Peebles, placing both hands on his desk, leaned back. Around the cigar in his teeth he said:

'If you do not agree, Mr Quinn . . . I very much doubt you will ride out of Stratton alive.'

EIGHT

I believed Peebles. He wanted me dead. If I had had any doubts that all of them were not in on the conspiracy, they now vanished. Not a man present spoke a word of caution to Peebles on my behalf.

'I don't see any point in continuing this conversation,' Peebles said. Then calmly he drew his pistol from its high-riding holster and aimed it at my head. I had sensed that this was coming, though it was sudden and the moment incongruous. I was already on my feet, Peebles still in his leather chair. Instinct more than thought propelled me up and over his desk, and as a shot from his .32 revolver sounded, echoing through the room, I hurled myself, shoulder first at the window behind the desk.

I heard a woman scream. Someone – Judge Manx perhaps – yelled out 'murderer!' I rolled through the shattered glass at the foot of the wall into the dark night, leaped to my feet and lunged into the cottonwood copse, seeing three faces staring at me from the lighted window. I wove my way through the trees and started toward the front of the house where my horse was hitched.

Slowly, painfully, I realized that the bullet Peebles had fired had tagged me. A searing pain, low down on my body, began to nag me. Touching it, looking at my fingertips, I saw that he had drilled me just above my right hip.

As if that knowledge slowed me, I began to stagger in my weaving run, my Colt now dangling in my left hand without my recalling drawing it. I looked behind me, my breath coming in tortured gasps, but no one was pursuing me from that quarter. I rounded the corner of the big house and saw two rough-shod men with rifles standing on the porch, their eyes searching the darkness for me.

My horse was gone!

Of course they had taken the big gray from me. I felt stupid, dazed. I was afoot in their town which was an armed encampment. I remembered Peebles's warning to me – I would not get out of this town alive. As I entered the alley that led past the brick courthouse toward the south end of town, and the stable where I might be able to snatch up another horse I heard the angry shouts behind me in a crescendo that rose to a whoop of pleasure. I had been spotted and they were after me in a minute.

I staggered on, holding my side which was bleeding more profusely than I had thought. My breath came in harsh gasps. My knees threatened to buckle with each stride. I could have turned and fired at my pursuers, but there were too many of them and I would only do them the favor of pinpointing my position. I staggered on, stumbling, once nearly going to the ground as I tripped over an unseen object in the dark alleyway.

Ahead of me now, stark against the surrounding black oak-trees, I saw Tabor's stable, where I meant to try stealing a horse. But the building was unlighted, its double doors closed. Cursing silently, I turned to watch the mob following me. They advanced slowly, no man willing to risk being to be the first to take a bullet. But they came inexorably, urging each other forward, and I knew that it was only a matter of time before they swarmed over me.

Desperately I tried banging on the locked stable doors. Hot blood leaked from my side, my hair hung in my eyes. The Colt was heavy as an anvil in my hand. It was no use. I turned my back to the tall double doors and braced myself for a shoot-out.

Then I heard a creak, rusty hinges shifting their position and a Judas door at the stable entrance opened, revealing a dark, faceless man surrounded by deep interior darkness. A hand reached out and touched my shoulder and I spun, crouching, my Colt cocked and ready.

'Get in here, Tom!' Barney Weber whispered desperately. 'Now!'

I followed the freckle-faced man into the interior of the barn. Did I trust him? No. I trusted no man these days, but there was little choice.

'Over here,' Barney said and he led me to a corner cabinet, head-high but only two feet by two in depth and width. 'Get in there. I'll get rid of them,' Barney said, and I managed to force my body into the small space where rakes and shovels hung. As I did so I heard Barney snap shut a padlock on the door's hasp. I was a prisoner now. I had to trust Barney, yet could not. I was beginning to get light-headed from exertion and the loss of blood. My side still flared with pain. I heard the pounding of fists on the double doors of the stable, and I waited, cocked Colt in my hand, the darkness around me nearly complete, the life dripping out of me.

'Open up!' I heard through the door of my hiding-place. 'Weber, are you in there? Open up!'

'Minute,' Barney replied sleepily. I heard the

creak of the hinges on the big doors and then Barney again, 'What's this about, men?'

'Anybody in here?'

'Been locked up for two hours. Nobody's here but me. Why, what's up?'

No one responded. Someone said, 'He must have made for the dry gulch. Trying to hide out there.'

Someone muttered a reply which I could not hear through the planks of the tool shed. After a lot of mumbled consultation and savage cursing, the posse made its way up the street, voices fading to silence. I heard Barney on the other side of the door say:

'Give it another ten minutes, Tom. Make sure they're gone.'

It was more like fifteen minutes, seeming like an hour, as I stood cramped, cold, my fury building before I heard Barney insert his key in the padlock of the tool-bin door and swing it open. He looked frightened out of his mind, his knees were wobbling with fear and yet he had done what he had to save my skin. It gave me a new respect for him. I told him that and thanked him sincerely.

'Tom,' Barney said, 'you always treated me right. The problem was, as you know, I was just never cut out to be a fighting man. I'd like to apologize for—'

'I don't need an apology,' I said. I was still holding my side. Blood could be seen leaking slowly through my fingers by the dull light of a kerosene-lantern hanging on the wall of the stable, and my faded red shirt was stained with deeper crimson.

'I've some new linen,' Barney said. 'Tabor uses it when he plasters a pony's bowed tendon. Let me get a roll of it and we'll wrap you up as tight as we can.'

Gratefully I followed Barney into a tiny room which seemed to be where he lived. There was a narrow cot with a tick mattress, a well-thumbed magazine, a chipped cup on a scarred table and little else. I stripped off my shirt and let Barney wash and bind my wound. Shivering in the night, I asked him through chattering teeth:

'Is there any way I can borrow a horse from you?'

'How about your own horse?' Barney asked with a grin that was weak but satisfied.

'My gray!' I asked in astonishment.

'Yeah. There was a runction up the street near the Peebles' house. I saw your gray come loping away. A couple of men tried to catch him up, but he was having no part of it. After the fuss died down I called to him. He knows me, of course, and I led him over here.'

'He's in the stable?' I grunted as Barney cinched me up with his bandage.

'No. That didn't seem like a good idea. They'd have found him here, and lain in wait for you. I picketed him in the oak-grove out back. That's how I knew I should watch for you, guessing you'd be coming along sooner or later . . . if you could. I knew you'd be needing a pony.'

'You're a marvel, Barney.'

'Maybe.' Barney sheared off the end of the bandage roll and stepped back. 'I'm sorry about all of this, Tom. For the way I ran. Maybe some day . . . when things are settled. . . .'

'I'll have a place for you, Barney,' I promised. 'When things get settled.'

He smiled briefly and I saw his old nervousness returning. 'There's a back door,' he said hastily, keeping his eyes averted. 'It's best you slip out quick before someone comes back.'

I agreed. The back door, which was hidden behind a stack of hay and feed-sacking, was apparently seldom used. Barney cleared the clutter away, and with a brief, uneasy smile, he swung the door open. I moved cautiously out into the chill of night. I worked my way into the oak-grove, seeing now a group of torch-carrying men on the far side of town, scattering weird angry shadows as they moved. Looking, I assumed, for me.

In a pained crouch I worked my way through the massive old trees. I whistled once, waited and listened and whistled again. That time I hear a horse nicker and stamp impatient feet and I knew I had found my gray.

I stroked his warm neck, painfully dragging myself up into the saddle. I sat my horse uncertainly for a moment, pondering as the faintest hint of light beyond the western mountains offered notice that the rising moon would be taking its place in the sky before long. Anyone recognizing my horse would be instantly on alert. However, being without a horse was a much greater risk. When my work was done I would need to be quickly away from Stratton. I kneed the gray and we started slowly through the back alleys of the town.

I had been arguing with myself all the way down the long trail as to whether or not I should actually do what I was planning, but the reception I had received, the bullet that had creased my side but surely had been meant to kill me had hardened my resolve.

The damming of the river would certainly kill Stratton. In time. But the anger riding with me now had tilted the scales toward sudden vengeance. I would destroy this town sooner rather than later.

The brick courthouse was silent. A single light gleamed through the window of a first-floor office. No one was on the streets. They were either in the saloons getting drunk or out roaming the wash with their torches, looking to shoot me down. I scouted the building out as I circled it and ended up hitching the gray outside a back door which stood slightly ajar, letting a sliver of yellow light leak out into the alley. Then I hefted my heavy saddle-bags, shouldered them and entered the building.

It was going to be a hell of a night.

There was a certain sort of blind madness settling over me. A hatred without anger, the need to destroy with no compunctions attached to it. My boots clicked down the hallway of the courthouse. At a cross-corridor I glanced up and down, seeing the barred cubicles. The city jail.

There was no one occupying any of the cells. You had to do a lot to be arrested in Stratton.

Opening each door as I passed, I made my way through the empty building. Everyone seemed to have gone home or was attending Shelley Peebles's party . . . or was out searching for me. I shifted my heavy saddle-bags from one shoulder to the other. My side continued to ache, to bleed, staining the white bandage to deep crimson.

The last door on my left along the corridor – the one I had seen light shining from – was partly open. Drawing my right-hand Colt I stepped through the doorway. A man in a dark suit, his tie loose sat there looking up at me. He wore bifocals; his dark hair was marcelled and plastered into place. He watched me with startled eyes as I approached.

'Who in blazes are you!' he demanded.

'Are you the mayor?' I asked.

'Certainly,' he replied as if my ignorance was an affront to his dignity.

'Put on your coat. Go home. Don't look back,' I said, showing him the muzzle of my .44.

'You can't come barging in here . . .' he began. He looked at me more cautiously then. I don't know how much he could read of the anger in my eyes, but the sight of a bleeding man, hatless and unshaven, twin Colts at the ready, gave him pause to consider his position. 'See here,' he said calmly, 'we can't have this, you know?'

'We have it,' I said solemnly. I let my saddle-bags drop to the floor, keeping an eye on the mayor, my right hand on the grips of my dangling Colt. 'You've got to pay attention to good advice when you're given it.'

I crouched down, opened my saddle-bags and saw the mayor's eyes open as wide as saucers as he recognized the dynamite in my hand for what it was. 'I'd go if I were you,' I said again.

He rose unsteadily, gawking at me, his eyes magnified through his spectacles. Nervously he began to warn me as I fixed my fuses, thought better of it and said only: 'When Mr Peebles hears. . . .'

I smiled crookedly. 'Oh, he will hear, Mayor. I promise you that.' Then I growled. 'Get the hell out of here unless you want to be blown to dog-meat!'

Neglecting his overcoat he sidled past me and rushed toward the door, his legs moving as if they had been affixed haphazardly. I whistled softly to myself and continued with my deadly work.

How much time had I? Two minutes? Five minutes? How long would it take for the mayor to rush to Peebles's manor and get help? No matter. I was finished with my fusing and out the door before a minute had elapsed, and the threatening, asplike hiss of the burning fuses had begun as sparks slithered along their length toward the dynamite bundle.

I ran limping down the corridor toward the back door of the courthouse. The mayor had left it open wide as he fled. I was nearly as frightened as he was. Fuses are not that predictable, no matter how many times you have used them. Some fizzle, some burn hot due to imperfect priming. I had seen more than one hard rock engineer fatally fooled on the railroad line. I swung into the gray's saddle and turned his head toward the forest verge, weaving through the stumps the town-builders had left behind in their clearing.

I ducked low to avoid a low-hanging bough and heard the familiar grumbling of explosives – a *whuffing* sound like the inhalation of powerful lungs, the bunching of a bellows before the explosive outward thrust began. I kept on riding, hard.

Then it came. The blast panicked my horse, shivered through the pines, sent a wave of heat across my back. I reined in. I wanted to see it. The impulse was too strong to ignore. Turning back, I saw the courthouse go up in a wash of flame. Fragments of bricks flew hundreds of feet into the air. The deep-throated boom of the explosion rattled my eardrums and erased any other sounds from the town. Red dust drifted in a huge smoky storm across Stratton, enveloping it in a choking cloud.

I wanted to smile, to laugh, but strangely there was no thrill in the aftermath. As with the destruction of the Sentinels, there was no joy in the destruction of men's labors. Nor in those of nature.

'Let's go,' I said harshly to the gray who twitched his ears as if to ask, 'What did I do?'

I was almost through with my night's work. Working my way along the north end of town I was nearly alone. The entire town had rushed to the scene of the destroyed courthouse. No one went too near, perhaps fearing a secondary explosion. Still they were drawn as if by irresistible impulse to the scene of destruction. I rode the alleys carefully, watching every moving shadow, and eventually swung down behind the telegraph office.

I found the telegrapher, a narrow, stiff man wearing a green eyeshade, watching the fire which still colored the sky over Stratton through the front window.

'What do you think happened?' he asked me without turning his head.

'No telling. Probably they'll find out come morning.'

'I suppose,' the telegrapher said, clicking his tongue. 'Too bad – that was sort of a symbol of civic pride around here. No town for a hundred miles in the Territory had a brick building.'

'It can be rebuilt,' I said, going to the counter to wait for the man.

'Yes, but you know how long it takes to get bricks and glass shipped out here.'

'I do.' I had been writing my two telegrams on the yellow paper provided for that purpose. Only now did the telegrapher seem to notice that the rough man before him wore a torn shirt, bloody, hastily wrapped bandage, was hatless and dirty.

'Say, what happened to you, mister? Were you near to the courthouse when it went up?'

I grinned. 'A little too close. I was just talking to the mayor, on my way out the door when the blast went off.'

Now the telegraph man's eyes narrowed. I shoved my wires across the desk toward him. He scanned them quickly and said, 'I can't send these,' much as Brian Gerwig had insisted at the newspaper office.

'Sure you can,' I told him, placing my walnut-handled Colt on the counter. I smiled without showing him any teeth. 'And I'll wait here for confirmation that they have been received, if it's all right with you.'

The stone house stood alone and still in the soft glow of moonlight. I rode my horse past it on whispering hoofs to the stable where I put the gray up. Removing the saddle was an agony. My side felt ready to explode. Fresh hot blood leaked down, into my trousers and boot. I leaned my head heavily against the horse's back and waited for the dizziness of pain to pass.

I was aware suddenly of a moon-silhouetted figure in the doorway behind me. I reached for my gun and half-turned.

'Tom?'

It was Julia Holt, I saw now. She had pinned her red hair up and wore a pale-blue shawl around her shoulders. She walked slowly toward me, frowning, 'You look like you could use a little help, Tom.'

'I'll manage.'

'That's one of your problems, Tom,' she said, 'always has been. You insist on doing everything alone.' She removed her shawl, folded it carefully and put it aside. Then she hefted my heavy saddle and placed it over a stall partition. I watched as she climbed up the wooden ladder, skirts hoisted, to fork down some fresh hay for the gray. I had twice begun to argue with her again, but found I hadn't the strength or the inclination.

When Julia had come back down from the loft she stood looking at me, her brows drawn together. 'Where did they get you, Tom?'

'Here,' I said, continuing to hold my wound as

if that could stop the bleeding. 'It's not too bad.'

'I can tell,' Julia said with faint mockery. There was perspiration on my brow, blood leaking between my fingers, and my legs wobbled once. 'Come on into the house; let's see what I can do.'

She turned from me and started away. I blurted out something that had been on my mind for a while. 'Julia . . . why have we never talked, why have you always been so distant?'

Without turning toward me she answered evenly: 'Tom, all the way on the long road West you had another woman, remember? And besides, I was much too young for you – you never even glanced at me, although I hoped you would.'

I couldn't think what to say for a minute. Carrying my rifle, I limped toward the stable door. Tightly wrapped in her shawl again, Julia turned to face me as I drew even. I looked down into her pretty, young, determined face, and thought that I must have been a damned fool. This was a woman of the West, a helper, a girl with fine instincts.

I touched her arm lightly, without gripping it and told her, 'You're not so young any more, Julia, and I have no other woman now.'

She half-smiled and then let the smile fall away. She looked into my eyes by the moonlight, nodded and walked away, leaving me to follow if I chose.

The unmistakable, remarkable smell of roasted beef greeted me as we walked up onto my porch and entered the stone house. George and Toby Trammel, looking satisfied with themselves, were sitting at the table. I dropped the bar on the door and placed my Winchester in the gunrack.

'Made it back, did you?' Toby asked with a smile.

'That *is* roast beef, isn't it?' I asked, glancing at their empty plates. Looking toward the stove where a blue roasting-pot sat. They nodded complacently. 'Where did it come from?'

'Well, Tom,' Toby said genially, 'you did post that notice – the one saying that unauthorized cattle being found on this land were subject to seizure or slaughter. I found this stray down near the notch and I figure he fell into that category. I sort of seized him and George took care of the rest of it.'

I grinned. 'Cut me a slab, will you?'

'Not just yet,' Julia said in a proprietary voice as George rose. 'First thing, mister, is we're going to see to that wound. Then you can eat.'

'Wound?' Toby said, and it was only then that he noticed the shape that I was in. 'God, Tom! There you go again. What happened?'

Julia hooked her hand under my elbow and said, 'He'll tell you later. One of you see if you can find that bottle of carbolic, and something to use for clean bandages. Oh,' she paused and her brow wrinkled in thought, 'also if you'll dig into my carpetbag you should find needles and waxed thread.'

'I don't like the sound of this,' I told her as we limped down the hall toward the bunk-rooms.

'Tom, you might not know this, but without saying so, out in the stable you invited me to take care of you.'

'I said no such thing!' I protested.

'You did. I know. A woman knows.'

'I have,' I said with a sigh, 'created a monster.' But I did not complain as, leaning on her slender shoulder, she walked with me into the bunk-room. I found myself secretly, unexpectedly pleased to accept her ministrations.

'Now what, Tom?' Toby asked as I shoved my empty plate away at last and we sat around the table sipping coffee. I had told them briefly about my meeting with Peebles, about blowing up the courthouse.

'I heard that rolling thunder,' George had said, 'and thought it was going to rain at last. But I stepped out onto the porch and saw nothing but starlight. Not a cloud in the sky – except for a low, flat haze over Stratton. We sort of figured what you'd done.'

Toby and George waited for my answer to the question. I told them carefully, 'It may really be time for you to pull out now. If we had fears that Peebles might send a gang of his gunmen up here before, now it's a certainty. George and Julia are not implicated, and they can slip away without. . . .'

Julia laughed out loud. I turned to see her leaning against the stove, a wooden spoon in her hand. 'You still don't hear what I'm saying when I talk to you, Tom! I'm not moving an inch.'

Toby grinned and reminded me again about his own vow to stick.

'What about the telegrams you sent?' George asked hopefully. 'Won't they do us any good?'

'I can't be sure,' I answered honestly. 'I sent two. One to the US marshal's office in Denver, advising them that we had a range war going on down here, that there had been killings and destruction the local law wouldn't – or was unable – to control.

'The other went directly to the governor. I told him that the whole territory is in chaos, that we needed help immediately.'

'Well then. . . ?' George said.

'It was late when I sent the wires, George. With any luck those telegrams will cross their respective desks sometime tomorrow. Assuming they are in their offices to read them. Then there's the time it will take the governor to make a decision to invoke martial law, the days it would take for any deputy marshals to ride all the way from Denver to Stratton . . . it could be weeks, it could be never.'

'I see,' George said gravely. He looked old for his years now. After the murder of his brother, Randall, and his mother's death, we seldom saw him smile. I was hoping that he remembered what I had told him about being responsible for Julia now, she having no one else. Hoping that he could think of some way to persuade her to flee.

Perversely, hoping he could not.

George asked his sister for another cup of coffee which she supplied, leaning so close to me as she poured that I got a dizzying whiff of her lilac powder. I was losing my mind! She had to be taken to safety. She was staunch and sensible, much too fine for me in the best of times. I couldn't let my personal wishes block the reality of what needed to be done.

Julia had bound my side so tightly that breathing was an effort. The burn of carbolic against my wound was a lingering memory, the stitching of my flesh which had caused tears to rise to my eyes provided a raw, throbbing reminder of events. George spoke again, putting his coffee cup down.

'I figure, Toby, that we should have one man in the forest at all times. . . .'

'Wait a minute!' I interrupted, but Toby joined in, answering George.

'I agree. We'll need to know when they're coming. And from the slopes a man could pick off two or three of the gunmen before they ever reached the flats.'

'Just a minute!' I said again.

'Then, before they could cross the dry creek, the look-out would still have plenty of time to slip down from the woods and into the house. Make sure we have spare boxes of cartridges on each of the window-ledges.'

Julia did not speak. She poured me another cup of coffee. I was tired, beat up, angry.

And extremely grateful to all of them.

'What do you think, Tom?' Toby inquired.

'Hell, don't ask me. I just live here.' I grinned despite myself and rose a little unsteadily. 'If no one minds, I am more than ready for bed. If you think you can get along without me.'

NINE

They came after us at the first light of dawn. The sun was no more than a seam of brilliant gold along the eastern horizon. The tips of the high peaks flushed rose with its reflected glow. George Holt, who had spent half the night standing watch in the forest, rushed in breathlessly, interrupting our first cup of coffee.

'They're coming, Tom!' he said excitedly, his young face taut with fear.

Toby leaped to his feet and was already strapping his gunbelt on, reaching for his coat.

'How many?' I asked, rising stiffly, more slowly than Toby by far. The night's sleep had done little to revive me. My side was, if anything, more painful than it had been the day before.

'Fifteen, maybe twenty. Tom . . .' he asked, his eyes desperate, 'what do we do?'

'We fort up and pick them off one by one,'

Toby Trammel said, but I shook my head.

'No, Toby. Saddle up our horses. We're pulling out. Peebles is serious this time. Sooner or later they'd figure out a way to assault the house.'

'Pull out!' Toby was shocked. It was the last thing he had expected from me. Julia had already shrugged into her sheepskin coat and was on her way out the door, scarf over her head.

'Get with it, boys,' I said, strapping on my own guns. 'We're headed for the high country.'

No one offered any further argument. Limping toward the stable, I glanced down the long valley and saw, distantly, the tiny dark figures of approaching riders. The rim of the sun was beginning to lift itself above the ranks of pines now, sending long shadows out from their bases. With Toby's help I got my gray saddled and tightened down the double cinches on my Texas-rigged saddle. The others had already mounted their ponies.

'Just a moment,' I said while I tied my saddlebags on behind the saddle and lifted myself heavily into leather. I winced with the effort and saw the concern on Julia's face. I tried offering her a smile, but it was a weak attempt. I was hurting bad, and she knew it.

'Let's go,' I said, and ducking my head to clear the doorframe, I rode the gay out through the stable door. I turned northward, toward the high peaks along Pocono Gorge and Toby, riding beside me asked:

'Where in hell are we heading, Tom?'

'The Crag,' I told him as we wove through the tall trees, riding along the old Indian trail we had followed into the high country not that long ago. Bleak iron-gray cliffs began to flank our trail. Toby began to respond to my statement, changed his mind and studied me thoughtfully. At last he grinned.

'You would, wouldn't you?' Toby said.

'It's what they want, isn't it?'

Behind us Julia asked through chattering teeth, 'What are you two talking about?'

'Nothing,' I said, turning my head. 'George, can you see the raiders?'

'They're riding harder now, Tom. Five, ten minutes they'll be at the house.'

'All right,' I said. 'They'll spend some time searching the house and outbuildings. If they've a tracker with them, he'll eventually cut our sign and they'll start north up the canyon. Toby, George, when you can find a sheltered spot with a clear view down the slope, you'll have to nestle in and keep them slowed down.'

In fact, not far on we came to a huge clump of yellow, moss-streaked boulders where a man could hold off pursuit for a long time – as long as it would take me to do what I needed to do. No one would be eager to ride up onto the mountain knowing there were snipers up there.

'Aren't they coming with us?' Julia asked in confusion. 'What are you doing?'

'Want me to tell her, Tom?' Toby asked with a broad grin as he swung down from his pony. He took two boxes of cartridges from his saddle-bags and eyed the jumble of rocks, choosing his position.

George, less sure, followed suit. I saw a brief conversation between Toby and George, and the younger man's expression brightened.

'Does everyone know what's happening but me?' Julia asked, not with petulance, but with true concern.

'I'm sorry, Julia,' I said seriously, 'but I've been doing considerable thinking. Trying to calculate whether this can be done. Because if I make a single mistake, there may not be a one of us left alive to see tomorrow.'

We climbed higher as the sun continued to blossom into morning brilliance. Looking back once I saw the confused knot of raiders in my yard, milling around, waiting for new orders. The canyon fell away to our right 500 feet or more, the peaks above us rose to 12,000 feet, a crow mocked our passing, a cold wind licked at the trees. My gray horse, mountain-bred and thickly muscled, was beginning to flag slightly. Julia's dainty pinto pony showed signs of breaking down. Still we rode on, ever higher.

'I heard you tell Toby that you were going to give the killers what they wanted,' Julia said. 'What did you mean?' The wind folded back the brim of her hat and let a few strands of red hair drift over her forehead. She was determined, curious, ready. I sensed no sign of doubt or fear.

'Simple,' I told her, as I halted my horse on the ledge Toby and I had last visited less than a week ago. 'That's what they want!' I pointed at the blue expanse of the lake I had formed. It glinted in the sunlight, placid but wind-ruffled, stretching for miles behind the Pocono Gorge.

'You caused that?' Julia asked in a hushed tone.

'I did. But it has served its purpose. Now I mean to destroy it and let the river flow freely again.'

'But, Tom . . . won't that?' Her voice was awed, now revealing some fear.

'Yes,' I told her, swinging down. 'If anyone is in the way of the torrent when it cuts loose, they'll be swept away like toys.' I knew she didn't like the idea, there was something about it that seemed unfair, cruel. I said: 'It's that, Julia, or we wait for

141

them to catch up with us and shoot us all down. They, I assure you, will have no such compunctions as we have.'

Behind us now we could hear rifle fire. The raiders had found our trail and were riding north while George and Toby Trammel defended our position. Urgency spurred me on. True, the two of them had position, but we were far outnumbered, and numbers usually triumph in any battle.

I unslung my saddle-bags, checked the contents and started toward the dam I had formed by toppling the Sentinels. Julia still sat her horse, the wind racing past her, shifting coat-tails, hat and curls. She watched as I half-crept, half-skidded down the slate slope toward the dead monoliths.

I had the dynamite in my saddle-bags over my shoulder. I needed both hands to grab onto whatever outcropping or twig of dead gray juniper I could find. I was nearly at the level of the wide-spreading lake now; anxiety battled with grim determination inside me. There was no wiring, no plunges-box this time. There wouldn't have been time to set that up properly. I had lengths of coiled fuse in my saddle-bags and matches.

If I caught a length of bad fuse, had it fizzle on me as I was half-way up out of the gulch I would have no choice but to go back down and then, with the fuse shorter than desired it would be a mad scramble back to the bluff – assuming I could make it at all. I slid to a halt at the very base of the fallen Sentinels. Water seeped between the great stones through dozens of tiny fissures, forming sheer waterfalls in miniature. I had to climb up the face of the dam a little to find dry niches. I could take no chance on wet fuses.

Behind and above me I heard constant gunfire as Toby and George Holt tried to keep the Peebles riders at bay. My fingers worked slowly, as if they were frozen. I looked over my bundles of dynamite, wondering if there were enough left to do the job. If not I was just going to make a hell of a loud noise, accomplishing nothing. I wished I had not wasted my other explosives on the court-house. I could have used more dynamite now. This was no sure thing, I knew. Sweat dripped into my eyes. I looked up, thinking of the millions of gallons of water above me.

More rifle fire echoed up the canyon. The Peebles men had settled in somewhere below and were rapidly emptying their magazines at Toby and George. How long could my rearguard hold out?

'I set the detonators, uncoiled the lengths of fuse and stood stock-still for a moment, looking up at the hundreds of feet of slate I would have to scale. It had not been so bad coming down, gravity assisting me as I slid and scrambled along.

Climbing the face of the gorge was a different matter.

I started up, the coiled fuse over my shoulder. The saddle-bags I had abandoned. One way or the other, I no longer needed them. The stiffening wind seemed to be trying to swat me from the face of the cliff. My fingers searched for handholds, my boots scraping their way from broken ledge to broken ledge. I reached up for a clump of ragged juniper and tried to hoist myself upward, but the dead brush tore free from the decomposing rock.

I should have known better – the tree's roots could never have found firm purchase on this rocky cliff face to have expanded enough to support my weight. I slid down the slope, my hands and elbows scraped raw before my right boot-toe found a fissure by chance and stopped my descent. I bowed my head to the face of the cliff, took three calming breaths, and started on again, not looking back down the 500-foot drop below me.

It probably was not more than another half an hour, but it seemed like months, years, before I managed at last to throw my knee up over the rim of the ledge and roll onto the flat ground there. The wind had increased in strength and in chill, but I paid no mind to it. I was alive, safe for the moment. I rose shakily to my feet to find Julia there, holding the reins to both of the horses.

'What now,' she asked, looking fearfully down into the Pocono Gorge. I rose, my lungs still burning from the exertion.

'I've got to get down the trail and tell George and Toby that it's time to pull out, to get upslope as quickly as possible,' I said, surprised to find I was panting, not from the climb, but from inner excitement. 'Then, when you three are on your way out of here, I'll light the fuses . . . and see how good a hard-rock man I am.'

'You're not sure it will work, are you?' Julia asked, coming near, searching my face with her green eyes. I was honest with her.

'No.' I didn't think anyone, even the most competent of explosives men, could be sure. Those men, though, would always have a second opportunity if they failed in the first. I had one chance only. It was a desperate attempt, but what else were we to do? Ride as far and as fast as we could until fifteen or twenty men caught up with us and gunned us down? I shook my head without words, looking across the long lake, the stony dam I had created.

'Wait here,' I told Julia.

'You wait here,' she said firmly. 'I'll get George and Toby.'

'Julia,' I grabbed the bridle of her little pinto pony as she swung into her saddle. 'There's shooting down there!'

'Really?' She smiled at me with amusement. 'I hadn't noticed.' Before I could stop her, she turned her pony's head sharply away, out of my grasp and started through the pines toward the clump of boulders where we had left Toby and George.

The racketing of the rifles continued. I looked down the trail and then returned my gaze to the gorge. One chance only, and not a very good one. I gave up the pointless speculation. It was time to act, not to consider.

I crouched, snipping off the unnecessary lengths of the long fuses with my pocket knife. Then I drew my match-cylinder from my pocket, clustered a group of three matches together because of the cold twisting wind and struck them, touching fire to both fuses at once. I stood watching as they sparked to life and began their long race down the sheer side of the gorge toward the planted dynamite bundles.

Anything could happen to them along that path. Even assuming they were dry and clean, there was no guarantee that the dynamite would do the job. I just didn't know that much about calculating mass and blast angles and such. I had simply tucked my charges into the weakest-looking fissures I could find. It was my best attempt, and probably my last.

The firing down the trail had abated except for an occasional seeking bullet. The Peebles men would be in no hurry to storm the mountain yet. They would wonder what had caused the snipers above them to quit firing, but not many of them would be willing to be the first man blindly to charge the slope. They would be discussing the situation, most of them urging caution since their own lives were at stake.

I heard the horses before I saw them and then my three companions on three tired-looking horses emerged from the forest to join me. Toby Trammel was smiling, but it was a uneasy expression.

'You'd better light those fuses, Tom,' he told me with more than a little nervousness. I nodded toward the gorge. Looking down I could no longer see the slender fuses, determine whether they were making their inexorable way toward the explosives, whether they had fizzled out or hit damp ground. Toby's expression changed and he said, 'Oh.'

147

His eyes reflected a memory of the last time we had set off a charge in these mountains, of the deafening explosion, the column of fire and smoke, the hailstorm of stones.

'Then I guess we'd better get out of here,' he said knowledgeably.

Perhaps Julia and George had believed we would remain where we were and watch for the result, but Toby had been through this before and he knew what was to come – what I hoped was to come. I nodded to Tony, swung into the saddle of the gray and said:

'Higher up, then west, away from the blast. We're better off among the trees.'

'What if it doesn't work?' George asked with understandable unease.

'We keep riding,' was all I could tell him. Truthfully I had no secondary plan, and now the realization seemed to come over all of them that if the dam did not go, we were lost.

I nudged my gray forward, further up along the old Indian trail. I did not know where it led; I had never ridden this high along it before. It led *away*, however, and away was what we needed just now.

I kept checking my mental clock as we wound through the tall pines, hardly disturbing the chattering gray squirrels who bounced along from bough to bough. Toby and George looked frankly frightened. I couldn't blame them. I felt as if we were riding along the rim of a volcano, waiting to see what would happen next.

We came upon an overlook about an acre wide where I could see back across the lake toward the dam. There I reined in, wiped my brow and told the others, 'You three go on ahead now. I want to see what happens. If worse comes to worst I'll remain here to hold Peebles's crew off as long as I can.'

George was hesitant. 'Tom, we can't abandon you. Besides, I'd like to see what happens too.'

'No you wouldn't,' Toby Trammel, who had seen one of my efforts before, said quietly.

'It's no good that way, George,' I told him. 'If it works, it does; if not I'll buy as much time for you three as I can.'

'I'm not going,' Julia said defiantly, and she swung down from her pony to look up at me, hands on hips.

'Yes you are!' I said, swearing under my breath.

'You are a bossy man, Tom Quinn!' she said with patient strength, 'I hope you're not going to be like this down the years.'

I had no answer for her. I spoke angrily to Toby and George although I had no reason to be angry with them. 'Hit the trail, boys. You'll find out soon enough what's happened.'

Toby nodded, tightened his mouth and turned his hammerhead roan forward to follow the trail. After a doubtful moment, George followed, looking back at his sister. I was down from my gray's back, my rifle in my hand. I walked near to the rim of the gorge where the wind lifted, flattened my shirt against my chest and tugged at my hair. I only glanced at Julia. I was angry with her, too. Again I was not sure exactly why. I only knew I did not want any harm to come to the little red-headed girl.

She eased up beside me, not touching me although it seemed as if she was. High clouds, so sheer as to be nearly invisible slipped past and traveled across the lake's expanse, barely shadowing it. The sun struck sparks on the water.

'Tom,' Julia said hesitantly. Now she did touch my arm with her hand. I had been listening intently and now I heard the familiar crumping sound I had been hoping for, fearing. I grabbed Julia roughly and half-dragged her behind the shelter of a small group of granite boulders. With astonishment she looked up at me as I threw her down onto the cold earth. 'What. . . ?'

I didn't have to answer. The first small rumble was a familiar sound to me. The detonators had caught spark. I didn't have the time to explain matters to Julia, for the second, vastly more violent explosion followed upon its heels and, nearly simultaneously, third. Both of my charges had caught.

The explosions were ear-shattering. The dark earth beneath us trembled. We were far from the blast site, but still small stones carried our way on a plume of red-streaked gray smoke and rained down, pelting us like spent musket-balls. Julia's courage had not flagged, but she wore an expression of incredulity.

'I didn't know,' she gasped. 'I've never heard anything like that.'

I listened, understood, but didn't take the time to respond. The explosion was all very fine, but had it served its purpose? I rose, leaving Julia behind and strode to the canyon rim. I could see the lake waters quivering slightly, like an uncertain beast. Still the fallen Sentinels held. I felt crushed and impotent. That had been my best shot, and it had failed.

'Tom,' Julia said, pointing below us. 'Look at the far side of the dam!'

I did and saw what she had indicated. A trickle of water, a freshet, had begun to flow over that end of the dam, like a living creature trying to find its way. Then, almost with warning, the ancient stone of the fallen Sentinels broke free, crumbled and crashed into the canyon and the lake waters broke free.

The waters surged, coursed and gathered momentum and the entire top of the dam broke open. The water frothed, turning white in its fall, changing in a few moments from a waterfall to deep rapids to a flood of Biblical proportions, a churning, boiling wall of water thirty feet high or more, funneling through the Cleft toward the wide valley below like a vengeful uncaged beast.

Julia had slipped her arms around my waist as I stood watching the havoc I had unleashed, rifle still dangling in my hand, the wind coldly calm, the lake slowly diminishing as the water below us flooded southward.

'Well, Tom,' she said, 'you did it.' Her eyes were thoughtful as she watched the raging river in the gorge. 'Still,' she told me, 'I can't help thinking about those men down there. All dead now.'

'I think about them, too, Julia. But there was no other way to stop them, and,' I pointed out, 'the only reason they had for being in the path of the flood was that they had taken gold from a criminal to ride us down and do away with us. If they had done their job, I do not think that any of them would be sitting around a camp-fire, regretting the taking of our lives. They would consider it a job well done and continue with their next murder.'

'And you, Tom?' Julia asked, looking up at me, holding me closer.

'I'll continue to think of them for a long time, but it won't be with regret.'

'Tom,' she said, leaning her cheek against my chest, 'can we go home now?'

Home. The word had a strange, comforting sound to it. I hadn't ever had a real home, even when I had returned to Stratton Valley I hadn't felt as if I was coming home. But with Julia. . . .

With Julia.

I heard the horsemen approaching and spun that way, Julia still clinging to me. It was George and Toby Trammel riding in. Toby was grinning, even the morose George Holt had a smile on his face.

'I knew you could do it, Tom!' Toby said with wild exuberance. 'We were about a mile up the trail when it went up, and . . .' He looked at me, at Julia who was at my side, her arms tightly around me, her head on my shoulder and he shrugged. 'Well, I guess we can talk about that later. George and I probably should ride along now to check up on the house.'

I nodded agreement.

'I'd appreciate it, boys.'

I placed my rifle on the ground, watched as the two men started down the trail again, then turned

Julia to face me. 'It seems we have some things to talk about later, too.'

'It seems,' she agreed, turning her face up to mine. The man behind me said in a slow drawl.

'I want to talk, too, Quinn. But I mean to do my talking now.'

The gunfighter, Kit Stacy, stepped from the forest verge, his hand on the butt of his holstered Colt.

TEN

Gently, but firmly, I nudged Julia away. The gunfighter advanced, his smile thin and set. He wore his buckskin shirt and pants and, incongruously, the ruffled white shirt he had sported at the fancy ball at Peebles's mansion. His face was streaked with dirt, savagely scratched on one cheek. His long blond hair, so carefully brushed the last time I had seen him, fell in lank disarray across his head and shoulders. There was no anger in his eyes, only cool determination.

'Caught up with me, did you?' I asked.

'Nothing to it,' Kit Stacy said, his eyes flickering from point to point, assuring himself that there was no one else around. 'You weren't trying to hide. I left the main body of men dithering and balking. I work alone, you see. It took a while, but I came up the far side of the ridge away from all the rifle fire.'

'It's all over now, Stacy. What's it to you what happens from here out?'

'I got paid for a job,' the gunman said as the wind twisted his straggly hair and the river roared through the gorge below us. 'It's bad for my reputation if I don't follow through on a contract.'

'Is that all there is to it?' I asked, watching from the corner of my eye as Julia edged away. The gunman nodded.

'That's all there is to it. If I don't complete my contracts, I don't get hired again. People want to know that I can be counted on to finish what I start.'

There was no sense in talking further with the man; I could see it in his eyes. He wanted to gun me down – one more small chore – and be on his way to his next job. He shifted just slightly, repositioning himself. I knew what he was doing. Turning sideways in a duelist's stance to offer a slimmer silhouette. I saw that, recognized it for what it was and also knew that it meant he was ready to draw down on me. There was slight movement of his hand, the tiniest of twitches and it happened.

'I've got you in my sights!' Julia cried out although she had no gun. I saw Kit Stacy hesitate slightly, glance toward Julia and draw at the same time.

It was enough a distraction, enough of an edge. I could never have matched the hired killer in speed, but the hesitation had broken his focus and when he brought his gun up I, although a split second slower, was able to fire first. At that distance, gunfighter or not, I could not miss and my .44 drilled Kit Stacy through the center of his body, sending him staggering, sprawling backward, his revolver discharging twice into the ground.

Panting, I approached his still form, my own Colt cocked and ready, but he did not move. His eyes were open to the long skies. Kit Stacy would not make it to his next job.

Julia came to me and hugged me tightly. She was shivering and so was I. It might have been the cold, the residual excitement or something far deeper, indefinable. I heard horses pounding up the trail and raised my revolver again, but it was George and Toby Trammel who burst from the woods, their ponies at a dead run.

'Tom! We heard . . .' Toby began. Then he saw the still, dead form of Kit Stacy against the cold dark earth and simply added. 'Oh.'

'Now, Tom?' Julia asked. 'Now can we please go home?'

A week later a sad-eyed deputy US marshal with a

long, drooping mustache named Connor showed up at the ranch. He told us that he had three other men gathering up the rowdies and giving them a chance to drift or go to jail. Most chose to drift. With Peebles now gone there was no way for them to make a dishonest living in Stratton.

A new election was to be held within three weeks. The mayor had slipped away into the distances. An old warrant had been found for Judge Manx who in fact was not a judge at all, but a veteran con-man. He was being transported to Denver to stand trial for a variety of misde-meanors.

I had signed over a hundred acres of land to George Holt and Toby Trammel as I'd promised them, and they were busy trying to throw up a log cabin before winter set in. After a long discussion, they had invited Barney Weber to join them on their spread. The three intended to run cattle and had purchased a starter herd from Peebles's estate.

The bulk of the steers had been inherited by Shelley Peebles's widow, Mary Ford Peebles, along with the mansion in town.

Our own plan was to raise horses in the long meadow. Julia had suggested it first and I had agreed. With the town growing again, with new settlers arriving almost daily, there would be a market for horses as well as beef.

We stood now at dusk on the broad porch of the stone house, our arms around each other's waists, watching the fiery play of sunset against the snowy mountains and gathering storm clouds. It was going to rain this time; probably it would snow. We heard the distant boom of rolling thunder in the high passes and went inside where the fire glowed brightly in the hearth.

We had nothing to fear from the coming storm.